D1194823

boys & murderers

HERMANN UNGAR

Boys & Murderers

collected short fiction

TRANSLATED FROM THE GERMAN BY

Isabel Fargo Cole

Twisted Spoon Press / Prague
2006

ISBN 80-86264-25-4

The translation of this work was made possible by grants from the Foundation of the Jewish Museum in Prague and the Stiftung Kulturfonds, Germany.

CONTENTS

UNCOLLECTED STORIES

PREFACE

I owe the melancholy privilege, the happy duty of introducing this posthumous collection of Hermann Ungar's work to a German audience, to the fact that I was one of the first to recognize and call attention to the extraordinary talent of the deceased. Having championed his debut, *Boys & Murderers*, it would be wrong of me to stand by indifferently at the publication of his last, posthumous work — whose inner beauty and artistic appeal stir me still more than the qualities of his first collection did back then. Then all was hope, harkening, delight in the rising of an auspicious star, faith in life; today this life, endowed with such great gifts doomed to unfulfillment, lies in the earth.

Did we bet wrong, then, did our instinct fail our hope? No, I am not ashamed of having commended to life one who was doomed to die. Death is not a refutation, and it would take an irreligious, Philistine view of happiness and success to make life's blessing the criterion for what is worth loving. The deceased reflected profoundly, bitterly, and truly on victory and defeat, blessing and debasement. "Today I know," he writes in the introductory passage of one of the stories in this volume, "that talent swiftly grasps how easily it can serve every cause, and often its most telling trait is the ability to conform to the ordinary and find a moral justification for this conformity. Seen from a higher vantage point, the victors in life are generally the vanquished. The deaths of the failures shine at times with the nimbus of victory."

This text originally prefaced the collection *Colbert's Journey* (1930), published shortly after Ungar's death. See commentary to the stories.

That is what it means to see through appearances with incorruptible, magnanimous perspicacity, and if it is true that "you shall know them by their fruits," one can be proud to have pupils with such convictions. Only one thing is forgotten or passed over here, that the true victories of life's children often lie where the masses do not see them, that renown is neither a means nor a product of comprehension, and that life's victors are also in need of humanity — which admittedly means wanting everything at once.

In retrospect, it seems to me that I always sensed the doomed aspect of Hermann Ungar's art and being and that this very "instinct" was the source of my sympathy, the motive for me to champion the early manifestations of his nature. In his unlaughing comic sense, his sexual melancholy, in the bitter and often uncannily deliberate way in which he expresses his vision of life — in his mental and even his physical physiognomy there is a pallor, a fatal mark, an austere hopelessness. It takes no second sight to interpret this prophetically, and it prevents me from regarding his early death as an accident. It did not surprise me that *Boys & Murderers* was immediately translated and much noted in France. The French esprit harbors more irony toward the fit, more inclination toward noble infirmity than do we Germans, with Goethe's legacy of a robust aristocracy of life seated deep in our blood. Unquestionably, all that is death's is not noble, while all that is life's is not base. But we best show our conscience-driven mockery against even the highest forms of conformity by bowing to death's nobility.

There can be no talk of fulfillment here, of the grace of maturation and perfection; but before life dropped him with the carelessness which so often appalls and outrages our human sensibility, his spirit did manage to give more than might appear from what I have said above. Following the first collection of novellas, we have a novel of anguished power, *The Maimed*; we have *The Class*, less momentous perhaps, yet still in its distinctive style and vision an expression of the cultivated primal quality which we call art; we have plays whose success in Berlin and Vienna did not come from conformity to the norm. And though to rebuke fate for its carelessness would be to take after the king who had the sea flogged, one is tempted to reproach it with all the things in Ungar's melancholy oeuvre that woo life with such poetic ardor; it should have shown more favor toward such sensual fidelity. Take, for example, what his "wine-traveler" says in the pages to follow about the secret of his wares: "In old wine is the scent of all flowers, the rays of the sun, children's laughter, men's sweat, the vision of the summer landscape, all ripe and heavy as the breast of a nursing mother." That is the song of life. Art may be marked by death, but it is always love, always life. "You are an artist," says the wine-traveler, "in a different sphere than the poet or the musician, but like them raised by your senses into a deeper and holier communion with Nature, lifted up from the inert masses of those whose eyes are as dull as their ears, their nostrils, their tongues and the nerves beneath their skin." Ungar, too, was raised by his talent into a deeper and holier communion with nature — and it is these posthumously published stories which reveal this most vividly, showing perhaps more clearly than those published during Ungar's lifetime what potential for development was nipped in the bud by his premature death, and their publication, for us, is a true human indictment of fate.

What an immensely significant figure, this servant Modlizki in "Colbert's Journey"! This story is rightly featured at the beginning of this collection; it is a minor masterpiece and would occupy an honorable place within any classical oeuvre. The others do not have this roundedness; they are sketchier, fragments and intimations of an unrealized epic world — but one need only read "Bobek Marries" to sense what a hearty grip on life this melancholy talent had, what a grotesque sacramentalism of the sensual he could muster and what he could have brought forth!

Hermann Ungar was born in 1893 in the Moravian town of Boskovice to Jewish parents. The Ungars were a family of merchants and farmers, the father was a merchant with scholarly and philosophical leanings. Hermann graduated from the German Gymnasium in Brno, studied law at the universities of Berlin, Munich and Prague and received his doctorate in the midst of the war. As a lieutenant in the reserves, he took part in the war from start to finish, spending the first years on the front in Russia and Galicia, and was severely wounded. After peace was declared he spent a short time as Advokatur Konzipient then as a bank clerk in Prague, held for a time the position of a dramaturge in Cheb, entered the Czechoslovak Foreign Ministry in 1920 and was assigned to the Czechoslovak Embassy in Berlin as embassy secretary. He married a woman from Prague and became the father of two boys. Recalled to Prague in 1928, he contemplated abandoning his official career to devote himself entirely to literature. We are told of an automobile accident which severely upset his nerves, paving the way for the illness — appendicitis — which, diagnosed too late, operated too late, carried him off the following year.

Ungar had a pronounced sense of family and origins. In him the sentiment called love of country manifested itself as the conviction that the only proper and salutary sphere for a person is that of his origin and that it is a sin and a fatal mistake to exchange it for another. Never, he said in conversation, should people leave the native soil that brought them forth if they wish to live happily and in safety. He saw in every journey something thrilling and dangerous, a challenge to fate — a mystical fear which probably played a role in the conception of

"Colbert's Journey." He himself traveled to Italy and Paris, but admitted with rare honesty, and in contrast to the self-congratulatory bliss of the travel poets, that neither the blue south, the famous artistic sites nor the charms of the metropolis had much to say to him. For practical reasons, he best enjoyed life in Berlin, where he had friends and his sphere of activity.

He began to write early on, long before *Boys & Murderers*, but revealed his literary ambitions only to two or three friends. It was typical of his character that those less close to him did not at all regard him as an intellectually interesting person. His fellow officers saw him as a good fellow who enjoyed entertaining the others, often with little regard for his dignity. His bank and legal colleagues knew him as an ordinary coffeehouse patron and were quite surprised to hear of books that he had published and that had even been praised.

He worked hard. For personal reasons, the diary he kept during the last years of his life is unsuitable for publication in full, but a theater journal has published fragments which testify to his fanatical love of the literary art, to the burden of responsibility under which he wrote or hesitated to write, to his anxiety about his mission, the fear that his ability could fade, his work become mere craft. "During the war," he wrote, "the immediate peril of death faced me hourly, but when I prayed, I prayed that God should let me live only if I was chosen to be a writer." What piety! And I mean not his belief in God, but his belief in writing. — At another point, on September 30, 1928, he writes: "I have six months' vacation. In this time no one shall hear a thing from me. Either I will have created something real by then, or I will finish with everything. Perhaps not with life, but with art. But without it there is no life for me. That is the danger." — The fear for his higher self is identical to the fear for his life. Is such a thing still possible?

Incidentally, he also feared for his life on the purely physical level, a hypochondriac constantly running to the doctor. That was ultimately the cause of his early death. The doctors, made callous and skeptical by his eternal fancies, underestimated and misdiagnosed his fatal illness for much too long.

He died under peculiar circumstances. At the time of his acute illness his mother, who suffered from a severe eye ailment, was in the same clinic where his operation took place. The operation is kept secret from her, but she has a dream about Hermann's death. Her son lives several days more, given up for lost by the doctors, but himself hopeful. Then his attendant is changed: into his room comes a nurse whom he recognizes as a childhood acquaintance from Boskovice. With horror — for he sees it as an omen. The earth has sent this face from the homeland to meet him. He must die.

His last fantasies concerned the premiere of his play *The Arbor*, which recently had its fiftieth performance at Vienna's Renaissance Theater. He died on October 28, 1929.

Thomas Mann
Nidden, 1930

boys & murderers

A MAN AND A MAID

I grew up without parents. My father died soon after my birth. He was a lawyer in the provincial town where I was born and he was buried. I own nothing to remind me of my father but a letter to my mother.

After the death of my father, who even left my mother a bit of money, my mother, driven by strong passion or the thirst for adventure, left town with an engineer, abandoning me penniless in her apartment with a maidservant. I never heard from her again. A Canadian court later delivered the above-mentioned letter, her sole legacy, to my home town. I was six years old at the time.

It is obvious, or at least understandable, that nothing ties me to my deceased parents. To this day I do not know what it is to love one's parents. I lack the organ for it: I cannot even imagine the meaning of filial love; in others it leaves me unmoved. What I lacked and what I often longed for was a warm dinner or a roof over my head or a good bed, never a father or a mother. When I say "orphaned," I think of poverty and a hard childhood. Otherwise I have no associations with the word.

And so my mother had abandoned me, alone and penniless. The town had to care for me, and it did so by committing me to the "hospice" which a rich citizen had endowed. This hospice had four vacancies for old men and two for boys. I spent fourteen years of my life as one of these boys.

I was a new beginning. I grew up without tradition, with no conscious tie to the past. I learned nothing from my father, and unfortunately I inherited nothing from him either. I faced life without the preconceived, force-fed opinions and the drummed-in principles which I imagine are instilled by the very atmosphere of the parental home. Novelty astonished and lured me. And the attraction between the sexes, I feel, is somehow familiar to those who grow up in a family simply by virtue of seeing man and wife together and feeling the bond of love to a mother. Unprepared, knowing not even her fragrance, I was surprised by the awakened senses.

But these observations are taking me too far afield; I ought to tell it all one thing at a time. How the house looked, who lived there and what went on to happen.

The hospice was an old, dingy-green, gabled house with many windows, each casement with eight panes. At first glance the whole house made an extremely asymmetrical impression. I believe it was made of two separate buildings joined together. Two well-worn stone steps led up to the door, and to the left of the door stood a stone bench, if the word can be used for a stone slab scoured smooth by years of use and resting on two squat blocks.

I sometimes sat on this stone bench when I tired of playing with buttons and balls.

From within, the hospice looked no more inviting than from without. The steep, well-worn stairs to the second floor, the ramshackle door to the vestibule which made a bell jangle, the dark stains on the gray paintwork of the walls, none of that is conducive to bright childhood memories. I know that I never experienced joy in this house. I believe no one ever laughed in this house. With other children I may have been loud and boisterous when we played in the nooks and crannies of the old alley, or on the grimy square in front of the school. But when I entered the house my heart cramped with an oppression I feel within me even today when I think back upon the hospice.

From the vestibule a door on the right led to the apartment of the hospice director, and on the left a flight of stairs led up to the rooms where we lived. Only two or three times did I glimpse the apartment of our director, whom we called by his civil name, Herr Mayer. It had tablecloths, family pictures, a sofa and upholstered chairs. To me these rooms were the pinnacle of earthly luxury. And Herr Mayer was the happiest of men. Today I know that he, too, was a poor man dependent upon the charity of the hard-hearted.

The hospice itself, where I lived, was divided into four rooms. The first, entered by the stairway from the vestibule, was relatively large and had three windows. In the middle stood the long, oilcloth-covered table where we took our meals. On the wall hung a large picture of our benefactor; I was afraid of this picture. I dared only to glance at it surreptitiously and quickly look away. It seemed to me the benefactor had angry eyes. As if it galled him that I was living here from his benevolence. Unfairly, I held the benefactor responsible for my unhappy youth. If he hadn't endowed this house, I thought, I wouldn't be here,

I would be with my parents like the other children and I'd have enough to eat and nice clothes and a ball to play with. My hatred of this picture went so far that one time I crept into the hall, as we called this room, and hung a large cloth over the picture. I never would have dared to do that in the daytime, when I felt the benefactor's eyes upon me. The cloth remained hanging for several days. No one paid any attention to it. Until Herr Mayer noticed it and had it taken down.

Three small rooms opened onto the hall. Each room was meant for two people. A narrow bed stood against each of the two long walls, between the beds a small table. Two chairs, a few pegs in the walls and a black chest for clothes and linens, those were all the furnishings of our living quarters. We had to wash in a trough in the vestibule.

The windows of our room looked out onto the narrow street below and the irregular gables of the old houses nearby.

At the time I was growing up in the hospice, not all the vacancies were occupied. Not because no paupers were found to apply for them, no old men and no boys, but because the cost of living had risen since the endowment's establishment and the interest on the capital was no longer enough to cover the full number of vacancies. And so there were only three old men in the house with me. One place for an old man and one for a boy remained vacant.

Being the only boy was not to my advantage. I believe it was no coincidence that the benefactor chose this particular shared living arrangement for boys and old men. In fact, I am convinced that his aim in taking in boys was to combine benevolence with the practical goal of obtaining cheap labor. I can vouch for the fact that my labor was amply exploited. Early in the morning I had to brush the clothes and polish the shoes of the old men, Herr Mayer and his wife, whom I almost never saw; and for Stasinka, the maid, I had to fetch coal from the cellar, chop wood, carry water and run errands before going to school, already exhausted. And so I often regretted not having a second boy with me to shoulder half my burdens. I found it especially irksome to wait on the old men. Mayer and his wife I saw as higher beings. Mayer had been placed over me as my master, and I was happy to oblige Stasinka, the maid. But the old men: they were my own kind! They were no better than I! Why should I polish their shoes and brush their clothes, these filthy old men I despised?

With only four of us living in the house, one of the rooms was empty. We slept in the other two, Jelinek and Klein in one, old Rebinger and I in the other. I say old Rebinger even though Jelinek and Klein were also old: Rebinger was especially old. Every night I feared and hoped he would die. But he did not die. He was still alive when I left the hospice and looked just as he had always looked as long as I could remember.

With these people, in this house, I spent the days of my youth, except for the hours in school and the brief spells playing on the street with other boys. I was not an especially good pupil. I was a poor child, and worse still, I was from the hospice. That means a great deal in a small town where the teachers socialize with the families of children from respectable houses, giving private lessons and sharing numerous ties of a material and social nature. When I knew something, when I did my lesson well, there was never much fuss made, as there was over others. When I did something badly, as was more often the case, I was rebuked, at times — this the teacher dared only with very poor children — even beaten. What was more, my mother's sudden disappearance had given me the reputation of moral inferiority, and my schoolmates teased me about it, even circulating several mocking rhymes about me which followed me until I left the school. For all the inanity of these rhymes, they wounded me so deeply that I remember them to this day, though I have gone through things which should have shaken me more deeply and which I have forgotten all the same:

I run to my mother love,
For she is my flesh and blood,
Have you seen my mother here?
Oh, I must find my mother dear.
Now just imagine, what a fright,
My mother stole away at night.

The very tune to which they sang this mocking rhyme still rings in my ears.

In the breaks between lessons my classmates took their breakfasts out of their satchels as I stood and watched them wide-eyed. I adopted the habit of asking them for some of their breakfast, and sometimes this actually obtained me a piece of bread and butter. Usually, though, I got nothing, and was only laughed at.

And so school was not a pleasant change from Rebinger, Klein and Jelinek either. On the contrary, I hated going to school, even though it allowed me to escape the hospice for a few hours. For I felt that the three old men at home took kindly to me. They knew how important I was to them, how necessary. They would take care not to get on my bad side. Of course they disgusted me; I despised them, I hated them, I would have beaten them if I had had the strength. But at home that was just what I took pride in. There at school I was despised, mocked. Here in the hospice I was a necessary if insignificant member of society.

The only one of the old men for whom I could not help feeling a certain admiration was Jelinek. Every morning at ten Jelinek went to have his brunch at the inn. It cost eight kreuzers, as he always declared importantly. Long before ten we all began to feel a great agitation. Only Jelinek played it cool. All of us felt: any moment now Jelinek, hospice inmate like ourselves, would utterly humiliate us once again, and we waited with bated breath. Never in all their hospice days did Rebinger or Klein enjoy the good fortune of going "brunching." The inn where Jelinek went for brunch was nothing fancy, of course, but there, all the same, he was the guest, master, customer. Jelinek savored these moments before leaving us. He paced the hall slowly. Klein and Rebinger feigned supreme indifference. But Rebinger's jaw trembled with rage, and the spittle trickled from his toothless mouth and onto his jacket. Klein fiddled so furiously with the umbrella he was repairing — he had been an umbrella-maker, and sometimes people still asked him for minor repairs — that he almost broke the spokes. "Well, off we go, then," Jelinek would say shortly before ten with inimitable composure, and walk off with slow, dignified steps.

And then Rebinger and Jelinek gave vent to their rage. I think they took Jelinek's brunch as an affront to their dignity. They started telling stories, they outdid each other in describing revelries of their own against which Jelinek's inn, his eight-kreuzer brunch, the whole town paled in comparison.

Jelinek could afford it. Jelinek was in business. I always pictured that as something terribly mysterious, though Jelinek's business was certainly quite lacking in mystery. It consisted of his going from house to house to buy old bottles for a few hellers and then selling them to a dealer for a small profit. To me, Jelinek was like a wholesale merchant whose ships sail the ocean, laden with merchandise. Next to him, the occupation at which I watched Klein every day — his broken umbrellas — seemed pathetic and insignificant.

Jelinek, with his drooping gray moustache, his shrill yet hoarse, perpetually screeching voice, was the only one of my fellow occupants I felt some respect for. Klein was nearly blind, his weary eyes peering through bent spectacles. He never shaved. And he was always fiddling with an umbrella gripped between his knees. I sometimes felt sorry for Klein, going so far as to silently slide him some object his hands were groping for, something that had fallen to the ground or that he had mislaid. His patient placidity disarmed my hatred, which at times did not even spare Jelinek.

Toward Rebinger my heart was hard, relentless, unforgiving. His body, quaking ceaselessly from his knees to the tips of his fingers, his red, lashless lids, the watery eyes, his toothless mouth, in constant motion, a thin unbroken thread of spittle trickling from one corner, his continuous harebrained stammering, his whole human helplessness made me his enemy. I was a child and chained to this old man who soiled his bed at night and whose expiring life, with death closing in, seemed to fight a nightly battle one step away from me. Was I born an evil child, that this old man in his affliction touched nothing in my soul and that being chained to the agonies of this trembling body, this extinguished soul, was a harder fate for me, I believe, than a prisoner's eternal dungeon?

Behind the hospice was a dirty little courtyard with steps leading up to a garden. One of the peculiarities of this house was that it was almost impossible to go from one part to the other, one room to the other, without taking stairs. The garden was small. A few trees grew there, in the middle an old nut-tree with a wooden bench beneath it. It bordered on other courtyards and gardens, separated from them by a tumbledown wall about the height of a man. In the far corner of the garden, past the nut-tree, was a well with a bucket hanging over it; when the wheel was turned, the bucket descended into the well on a creaking chain. The water used in the house was drawn from this well.

In the afternoons Rebinger would sit on the bench under the nut-tree. His hands propped on his rough-hewn cane, he mumbled to himself. And when Stasinka came past, a bucket in each hand, Stasinka, the maid, her lusterless eyes gazing dully ahead of her, her sturdy feet in wooden clogs, shuffling, he would nod at her. His eyes were fixed on her fat heavy breasts, which wobbled at every step. I turned the wheel for Stasinka. And I saw Rebinger's eyes and Stasinka's chest and felt that Rebinger knew something unknown to me.

Without a word of thanks Stasinka went back the way she had come. Rebinger gazed after her, his sunken lips twisting in lecherous laughter. And the spittle trickled onto his dirty jacket.

For years I lived with Stasinka under one roof, and there is no doubt that I spoke to her a great deal. But strange though it may sound: however precisely I remember each movement of hers, her gaze, her gait, her body, however vividly her smell seems to fill my nostrils when I think of her today, I barely remember her voice. It is as if I never heard her speak, never laugh. In my memory Stasinka is dumb. I hear her breath, expelled through her nose with a snort, I see her fat colorless face, I see the very pattern of her dress, but I do not hear her say a word.

I might have been eight years old or a little older when Stasinka entered service in the hospice. I do not believe that Stasinka excited me in any way from the start. That must have happened little by little. When I think it over, I find that I might — might, I say — have passed her by in complete indifference if it hadn't been for Rebinger. Rebinger opened my eyes, and to this day I vividly recall the moment it happened.

I was in the garden, furtively gleaning half-rotten apples from the ground. Rebinger sat on his bench, squinting into the sun. Then Stasinka came across the garden with her buckets, heading for the well. I was a few feet away from Rebinger, and I saw his lips move, saw him tremblingly thrust his stick against the ground and make as if to rise.

"Oh, you fat kalleh, you," he said, pausing after each word as if to muster strength for the next. "you fat kalleh!"

I dropped the bitten apple to the ground. I saw Rebinger's contorted face and followed his eyes' staring gaze. Astonished, as if for the first time, I saw the maid. Rebinger's slurred words echoed in my ears: kalleh, you! I had never heard the word before. I knew nothing and everything. Something new broke in upon me when I saw her for what she was: Stasinka! the fat kalleh. I had never seen a woman but hard at work, never once in motherly tenderness. Now I was confounded by the upwelling of a dormant, untouched spring within me. I threw up my arms and fled.

I feel that the first impression of the awakening senses must be indelible. That each is forever enslaved by the first woman he meets, if only in a love which religion and morals have divested of passion, like the love for a mother. My passion toward Stasinka never faded, though Stasinka remained dull and lusterless, while I was to behold life's pinnacles.

The first consequences of the encounter in the garden were a seductive fear of Stasinka's presence and flaring hostility toward Rebinger. I sat awake in bed, my face contorted by fright, listening lustfully to the eruptions of his nightly pains. No doubt I would have let him choke to death on his coughs without calling for help. In vague foreboding I felt that Rebinger, that babbling, benighted old man, had wrenched my life from its path and delivered it up to guilt and destruction. Hatred and evil within me thrived on Rebinger's suffering.

Though Stasinka's presence, the sight of her, alarmed me to the depths of my soul and made my limbs tremble with the fear of something threatening and unknown to me, my dreams were filled with the yearning to see her. By day I lurked in the dark corridor so that her smell, her dress would brush me when she left the kitchen. I sat by the well and waited for her to come fetch water. When Rebinger sat on the bench under the tree I hid in the bushes and kept my eyes riveted to his face. I could not have stood before him unconcealed; my hatred would have turned murderer. All I had to do was jump up, and his throat would have cracked between my unyielding fingers, had not leaves and branches risen as a barrier between him and me. I fled into hiding from myself.

When she came I turned the wheel, trembling. She did not look at me. Her animal eyes gazed vacantly at the rolling chain. She went without thanking me.

But some power over me forced me pitilessly into her presence. Silently I began to do her chores for her. She stood or sat by, expelling her heavy breath through her nose, and acquiesced. But I glanced anxiously from the wood I was chopping to her full, pendulous breasts, slowly rising and falling.

I began earning my first kreuzers then. I did so by fetching newspapers from the post office on Sundays and delivering them to the subscribers; in our town the post was not delivered on Sundays. I earned about twenty to thirty kreuzers a week this way. I bought sweets with the money, a colorful ribbon, a shiny comb, and laid them next to Stasinka, who took my presents without a word.

Over time I had managed to gain admittance to the kitchen, which actually belonged to Herr Mayer's apartment. In the evening, when the Mayers had gone to sleep, I quietly opened the kitchen door and went inside. Stasinka stood there washing the dishes or preparing the next morning's chores. I went up and took the work out of her hands.

More time passed like that, a long time, it seems. And I grew up in the hospice with three old men and a maid.

The moment when, at fourteen, I had to leave the hospice cannot have been far when another incident imprinted itself on my memory with particular vividness.

It happened one evening in the kitchen. The little petroleum lantern burned on the kitchen table. Stasinka and I crouched on the floor, sorting lentils from a big washbasin. Stasinka sat very close to me. I did not dare to stir my arms or feet, barely to move my hands. Only my fingers, like alien apparatuses, picked the bad lentils from the basin. Stasinka's presence was like a physical burden weighing heavily on me and her and all things.

I felt her breath on my ear and cheek. My nostrils drew in the warm smell of her body. Like a big weary animal she crouched in the fullness of her sluggish flesh, her eyes lightless, her big hands next to mine in the basin.

My feet began to tremble. I felt as if my body were losing its hold and falling. But I was terrified of moving even a hair's breadth closer to Stasinka, as if then something monstrous, crushing would inevitably overtake me and destroy me.

I teetered. With a shudder, the resisting muscles' cramp

relaxed. I felt my shoulder draw close to hers, felt it as if I were covering a tremendous distance. Now my body touched hers.

But Stasinka pushed me away from her. And her hand hovered calmly over the lentils again.

At that, desire erupted within me. Boyish shyness fled. Animal, passion, blood cried out in me. I was free. I was ready to be master. For a few fractions of a second my hands groped helplessly at my head, then stretched out. I jumped up. Reached for Stasinka's full, fat, rising and falling breasts.

Stasinka rose without a word. She put her hands around me and lifted me like a light load. She opened the door. She drove her heavy fist into my ribs and dropped me to the ground at the threshold. Then she calmly closed the door behind her.

And I lay there writhing in the first raptures of love.

In my last months at the hospice I stopped helping Stasinka with her chores. I watched her and shadowed her. I no longer wanted to serve Stasinka. I wanted to be stronger than she.

I stood outside the kitchen door at night and listened to her peaceful, sated sleep. I pressed my ear to the door and eavesdropped on her human functions, shaking with forcibly restrained desires. I followed her into the cellar and waited for the hour when I could grab her, grab Stasinka by her fat breasts. But I feared the lusterless gaze of her dumb being.

And so the last days of my suffering in the hospice passed, convulsed by unfulfilled desires. I had already left school, and the day drew near when I would have to take leave of my childhood, go out into the world, alone, fending for myself, and see how I'd manage.

I did not find it hard to leave. All the more so as I was to remain in our town for the time being and my departure was not a final farewell. I could go to the hospice every day after work if the spirit moved me. But I felt nothing whatsoever for the house and its occupants, not even a sense of gratitude. I was glad to leave the house of my unhappy childhood, the old men and Herr Mayer, glad that I would no longer have to see the picture of my benefactor before me, and my soul was filled with images of a happy future in which, suffering no longer, I was master, raised above others.

Yet while I left, Stasinka the maid remained. I would no longer be able to sneak after her on her errands through the house, and outside the house her presence would no longer surround me. But one day, I knew, I would come back and stand before Stasinka as a master with power put into his hands, power over gold, over people, and I would laughingly wrestle her to the ground before me.

Two days before my departure, I was called to the trustee of the house, a respected member of the community. He made me a speech of which I understood little, distracted by the richly appointed room — or so it seemed to me — in which I was received. All I remember is that he admonished me to be remindful of the benefactor and his good deed in my future life and that, it strikes me now, he tried to reassure himself more than me about setting me out into the world helpless and alone, expounding that due to the seed the hospice had planted in my heart I would never lose my way in the life struggle ahead of me. For all his concern, he released me with a gift of ten guldens, established by the benefactor for boys leaving the hospice, and never worried about my fate again.

On the morning of my departure I got up as always, and as always I brushed the clothes and polished the shoes of Klein, Jelinek and Rebinger, and Herr and Frau Mayer. Then I said farewell to Herr and Frau Mayer. Herr Mayer said a few words to me, wishing me the best of luck and holding my hand all the while. I felt that he was the only one who was reluctant to let me go off into the unknown, and that he was now trying in vain to say something kind to me. Somehow I must vaguely have sensed his kindness, and with it the fact that I was, after all, losing a home, albeit a poor and joyless one, for I began to sob. And Herr Mayer kissed me on the forehead.

Then I went into the hall where the old men were sitting, wrapped my jacket in newspaper, gathered my meager possessions, shook hands with the old men and went. In the courtyard I stood below the kitchen window and cried:

"Farewell, Stasinka, I'm leaving this place, farewell!"

Stasinka's head appeared in the window and her eyes regarded me wearily.

I did not have far to go. The inn The Bell, where I was to start as an apprentice, was about five minutes from the hospice. I wanted to become a waiter. Of all the occupations that came into question, this one seemed by far the most promising, and it attracted me in a way I could not account for. Perhaps Jelinek's brunch, the scene in the hospice every morning, was to blame for lending a special appeal to a profession that entails spending all one's time in an inn. Whatever may have moved me to the decision: I apprenticed myself to Widow Glenen as a busboy.

The widow was an old gray-haired woman. She was fat and resolute with a slight squint. You could tell by looking at her that she was quite capable of coping with drunken guests and menials.

The long dark taproom made anything but a civilized impression. People with their hats on, the stink of pipes, spittle on the floor, yelling card players, on top of it all a nickelodeon trying vainly to shriek down the noise. In a corner Widow Glenen sat in state behind the little counter, surrounded by bottles, glasses and gleaming tobacco-pipes. Everyone leaving the room had to pass her, and she slid the proffered nickel or silver pieces into her drawer with a placid nonchalance.

My initial duties consisted of going from table to table to clear away the glasses after the guests had gone and washing them in a pail behind the counter, then running down to the cellar at a signal from Frau Glenen to fetch a bottle of something or other. On top of that I had to wipe the tables, stoke the fires, chop wood, brush clothes, polish shoes, in short, to do whatever had to be done at any given moment, while Franz, the older apprentice — under the stern gaze of Frau Glenen, who never took her eyes off him — filled the glasses which I or the guests slid over to him and saw to it that the stall and the yard were clean and tidy.

The work I had to do was not easy, and at night I was so tired that I sank down on the pile of straw I had made myself in the guest room and fell asleep. That was why I did not go back to the hospice at first, and barely even found time to think of Stasinka. Later, once I had gotten used to the work and learned to shirk this task or that, I would slip out of The Bell at dusk and sneak into the hospice garden the back way, through other people's gardens and over walls. Then I stood in the bushes and waited for Stasinka to come. When she came, I approached slowly and turned the wheel as I had in the old days. She acquiesced. She never seemed at all surprised. Then she went, and I gazed after her body, hips swaying slowly under the weight of the full buckets, until it disappeared into the house. I went back the way I had come.

The job in The Bell could not appeal to me for long. I had greater things in mind. I dreamed of crowded restaurants, flooded with light, the kind Franz, who had once been to the capital, had told me of. I saw myself dressed in a snug black jacket striding among tables where elegant people sat, and my pocket was filled with jingling coins. Franz was saving his money to travel to the capital and look for a job there, and I decided to go with him. But with the few kreuzers a servant sometimes gave me for helping him unharness the horses, I could not dream of saving up the forty crowns which Franz figured would be needed to begin with. I did not worry about the money question, though. And when Franz told me one night that he was going to set out in the morning two days later, I said I would join him.

I had no preparations to make. All that I owned, I carried on my person. I had no one to say goodbye to but Stasinka. That I would do on the very last night.

The evening before our departure Franz went to say goodbye to friends and relatives. I stayed behind. The house fell very still. Frau Glenen slept soundly in the third room. Only now and then, from the stall, came the clank of a horse tugging its chain.

I got up from my bed of straw and groped my way to the bar-counter without lighting a light. I went to the money drawer and slipped the blade of my knife into the narrow crack between the drawer and the countertop. Then I slowly began to lift the countertop. Unable to open the drawer this way, I started removing the screws that fastened the lock to the wood. Then I tried to work the lock loose in its setting. That worked. The drawer could already be pulled out a bit. Now with all my strength I braced the knife against the countertop again while pulling the drawer out with a violent jerk. The lock snapped and the drawer was open.

I took two hundred crowns in neatly-stacked bills and closed the drawer. Then I left the house to say goodbye to Stasinka.

Altogether I have stolen twice in my life. That was my first theft; the second I must speak of later. To anticipate, my second theft differed from the first chiefly because the second time I already knew I was doing wrong, while the first time I was quite innocent of the thought. At the time it seemed obvious to me that I could take the money from the drawer, as I needed it so badly. And today, now that I think differently than I once did about many things I have done in my life, I believe that with this first theft I really did no wrong; the ingenuousness with which I stole exonerates me before myself.

So I took the money and went to say goodbye to Stasinka. As I had so often done, I climbed over the walls until I stood in the hospice garden below her window. It was a warm summer night, and Stasinka's window was open. "Stasinka," I called softly, "Stasinka," and when nothing stirred I took a handful of sand and pebbles and tossed it through the open window.

Stasinka's head appeared, sleepy and tousled. "Come down," I whispered, "I'm going away. I want to tell you something, Stasinka."

She vanished. Several minutes passed in which I teetered fearfully between hope and hopelessness. At last the sound of her heavy tread on the stairs delivered me.

She stepped outside. Her body was just barely covered by a sheet.

"I'm going away, Stasinka," I said. "I've come to say farewell to you."

She said nothing. I moved in on her, emboldened by the knowledge that I would not see her for a long, long time, perhaps never again.

"I'm going away, do you hear," I said; I was standing very close to her now. "I haven't gotten even with you yet, Stasinka." I was enraged by the way she stood there dumb, impassive. "You can't pick me up like a child now, you, no you can't! Can't pick me up, you hear!"

I crowded her against the door. Stasinka gave way without resistance.

"Now I'll show you who's strongest this time, Stasinka! Want to see?" We were standing in the dark vestibule. I pulled the door shut behind us.

A dull glimmer from the barred window by the door fell

upon her form. Nothing could be heard but her heavy, even breathing.

Now I grabbed her tightly. She raised her hand to ward me off. "Trying, trying to push me away again, push me aside, huh? Stasinka? You!"

I slipped my leg behind her knee and laid her flat on the ground. Her eyes, alien and unmoving, watched me. I knelt over her. When I grabbed at her breasts she gave a sudden wrench and tried to break free. I went for her throat.

"You kalleh you, you kalleh," I said and flung myself upon her.

She raised her hand as if pointing upward. Her eyes gazed up fixedly as if beholding something frightful.

I turned around. And saw — pressed to the window, twisted in a saturnine leer — Rebinger's face.

I jumped up and ran outside. He stood gripping the bars with his hands. I came up on him from behind.

I felt as if my hands, closing around Rebinger's scrawny neck, were iron pincers. Voluptuously I felt his body's eternal tremor in my fingers. When it ceased, I dropped his body to the ground.

Then I went back into the house, liberated, as if I had done a great deed. Stasinka was gone.

I crept up the stairs. I knew that if the door were wrenched open suddenly its bell wouldn't ring. It made a quick soft noise.

The kitchen was locked. I scratched at the door like a dog. Then I listened and heard: the loud breathing of Stasinka asleep.

As I crossed the garden I saw Rebinger's form in the breaking dawn, staggering as he groped his way uncertainly along the wall to the house.

That was my farewell to the hospice and Stasinka. For the last time in a long while I climbed over the walls and crept through the gardens. I did not turn around. I strolled over to the train station.

In the city we took lodgings in a dark, dirty neighborhood. Three other men slept in the same room with us, different ones every night. In the daytime we went from hotel to hotel to offer our services.

For the time being, at least, Franz's plans were not as ambitious as mine. He started with the small hotels and was content to find, after four or five days, a job as a valet in a seedy establishment, said to be especially lucrative due to the hourly turnover. I could understand Franz's point of view. He had only forty crowns, while I had nearly two hundred left. I could afford to be choosy.

I had always pictured myself in a snug black jacket, hastening past tables where elegant people sat. I was not about to scale back my demands now. I would have relinquished the black jacket only for the livery worn by the self-possessed bellboys who stood in the lobbies of the elegant hotels. But to end up like Franz with rolled-up shirtsleeves, wearing a blue cap with gold letters — not for anything in the world.

So I went from hotel to hotel without success. Eventually I became less particular and began to offer my services in cafés and restaurants as well. Perhaps, like Franz, I would soon have become a valet in a third-rate hotel had I not made an acquaintance which spared me that fate.

Franz's bed was taken by a young blond man, and to my surprise, I found him next to me night after night. Small wonder that the two of us, the only permanent fixtures in the eternal flux of nightly guests, should strike up an acquaintance. I learned that my neighbor was called Kaltner, that he had lived in America for several years and saved up some money there. He had come to give his luck a try here, but unfortunately had realized that there was no money to be made and was returning to America in just a few days. The ticket for the crossing was in his pocket.

Kaltner told me about America. That you could make your fortune there if you were willing to work, and that if anyone asked him, he would advise them to go.

I was tempted by the prospects which, from what Kaltner said, America held in store for me. I let Kaltner take me to a café and introduce me to an elderly gentleman with a beard who scrutinized me through a gold-rimmed pince-nez which he propped for the purpose on the front third of his gaunt nose.

"Do you have a hundred and twenty crowns?" the gentleman asked abruptly after examining me like that for a while. When I said yes, he sat down at once and wrote something on a brown slip of paper. "If you please," he said. I put down a hundred and twenty crowns and he gave me the certificate.

It had all happened very quickly and without anyone actually asking me what I wanted. But even if I had wanted to, I would not have dared to contradict.

The next day I was on my way to Hamburg, and the day after that I boarded an old grimy ship called the Neptune.

I had nothing with me but three loaves of bread and twenty marks in cash.

Like my first train journey, my first voyage across the ocean made no impression on me. I seem to have been unreceptive to natural beauty, which will surprise no one who knows that I grew up in a hospice and realizes, after what I have told, what kind of childhood I had. Not to mention that I had no time to idly take in the scenery, as I came close to starving on the ship and survived only by carrying water for the wretched steerage passengers, helping wash diapers and the like, rewarded here with a morsel of foul-smelling sausage, there with a piece of bread or a swig of liquor.

One might imagine that living with the emigrants, those filthy, half-starved people, would have softened my heart toward human misery.

But the poverty of my fellow passengers moved me to revulsion and contempt. To be rich, I thought, to be powerful! And gold, plenty of gold in my pocket. And then to stand before Stasinka, the maid from the hospice.

That, it seems, was the only dream of my youth.

On the ship I had already learned that there were neighborhoods in New York where Germans and Jews lived and one could get by without speaking English. We arrived in the morning, and I was shown to this part of town by a fellow passenger who had gone back to Europe to fetch his wife. There I began looking for a job at once.

Luck was with me. That very afternoon I was a busboy in a small bar.

I was not happy there for long. I had a lot of work, unpleasant work, and barely enough pay to fill my stomach. Every day there were brawls, and at a signal from my boss I had to settle them by throwing out the guests. I soon abandoned this job, and after a stint of having different work every day, I ended up in a music hall where I stayed for several months. I had a relatively good time of it there. One of our girls, a tall slender thing about thirty years old with light blond hair, took a fancy to me, and I was able to pocket part of her earnings on top of mine.

All the same, I probably would have made no headway in America either, living out my days as a waiter, or at most becoming the owner of a small bar, had I not been bold and unscrupulous enough to lend fortune a helping hand. Having realized that I could achieve no more in our music hall than I already had, I left, simply absenting myself one day to avoid saying goodbye to my girlfriend.

I took a job as headwaiter in a bar with a great deal of high-stakes gambling, meaning that there was money to be earned. My job in this bar was a turning point in my life.

I had been at the Chicago Bar for about two months when, early one morning, my eye fell upon a fat, sleeping gentleman easily recognizable as a wealthy cattle-dealer or farmer. I stood leaning in the kitchen doorway. The sleeping gentleman was the last guest. Tired, I yawned and looked at the clock. It was four-thirty. I looked over at the bartender, dozing behind the bar, then back at the sleeping guest. My eyes lingered on his back. His jacket had ridden up slightly, and the outline of a well-filled wallet was clearly visible in his tight-stretched trousers.

I walked slowly past the sleeping man. I took the empty glass from the table in front of him and carried it to the bar. There was no doubt about it: both guest and bartender were fast asleep.

I took my knife from my pocket and slashed the man's pocket in passing. Then I went back to the kitchen door and leaned on the jamb.

The tear in the man's trousers gaped with every breath he took. A brown leather wallet, the kind rural cattle-dealers carry, bobbed up and down, coming more clearly into view with every breath. I did not move. My eyes circled ceaselessly from the guest to the bartender, from the bartender to the wallet.

After several minutes the wallet was almost fully visible. The top already protruded from the cloth of the trousers. Only the bottom held loosely.

I went up to the man slowly, seized the wallet with thumb and forefinger, and hurried out the door onto the street. To avoid attracting attention in my white waiter's outfit, I whistled for a cab and drove home.

There I opened the wallet. I found four thousand dollars in bills. Four thousand dollars is money, Stasinka, four thousand dollars is money.

At once I got myself ready to go, and was sitting in the very next train heading west.

That was my second and last theft. From then on I no longer needed to steal. In the wallet, along with the money, I had found the addresses of cattle-dealers in every state. I made use of my predecessor's connections and earned twenty-five thousand dollars in two years.

Now I sailed to Europe in a cabin.

There was no question that I would return to Europe. I was never a dreamer. I worked hard in America and had no time to dream of Stasinka. I thought of her and saw her shuffling walk, her big heavy breasts and her dumb animal gaze. I did not yearn for her: I knew I had to return to the hospice once more and become master over Stasinka.

One summer evening I arrived in my hometown. The train station had not changed a bit, but there was a new inn across the street. I took a room. At dinner I questioned the innkeeper and learned that at the hospice everything had stayed the way it was. Except that Jelinek, Klein and Rebinger had died. But three other old men had taken their place. I told the innkeeper, who seemed nonplussed by my interest in the hospice, that I had grown up there myself, and then asked openly about Stasinka. Stasinka was still the hospice maid.

When it was completely dark, I set out on my way. Again, just as when I was apprenticed at The Bell, I crept across the gardens and over the walls. I remembered every step of the way. Then I stood in the garden of the hospice. As in the old days, I tossed a handful of sand through the open kitchen window. Stasinka's head appeared.

"Stasinka," I said, "I've come to see you. Do you remember me, Stasinka . . . ? Come down to me, Stasinka!"

Stasinka's head disappeared. I knew she would obey. She

came out the door, again wrapped only in a sheet. "I've come to see you, Stasinka," I said. "Just look at me, Stasinka, take a good look at me. You see, I've made something of myself. Do you know what that means: to make something of yourself?"

Stasinka gazed at me submissively. She still had the same big pendulous breasts and she still expelled her breath loudly through her nose.

"You won't push me away now, Stasinka!" I said. I went up close to her. "Not now you won't. Now I'm a gentleman, Stasinka, understand, a gentleman!"

I put my arm around her. She stood there wearily.

My fingers reached for Stasinka's breast. But Stasinka stretched out her hands and calmly pushed me away. Her eyes were unmoving, fixed on the ground.

"Stasinka," I said, "I'm not a little orphan child anymore. Stasinka, now I'm stronger than you."

But Stasinka the maid turned away and, hips swaying slightly as if she were carrying the heavy buckets to the well, walked slowly to the door.

I'll break you yet, I thought, I'll break you!

"Stasinka," I said, making an effort to speak calmly and kindly. "That's not why I came to see you, don't be afraid, that's not why. I wanted . . . I wanted to take you with me to America!" She stopped at the door. And I began to tell her about America. I didn't know what would tempt her, what she would understand, so I described everything out of order. I began with the beautiful dresses she would wear. I spoke of the quiet life she would lead. I spoke of money, of food, and once again of food.

Suddenly I was set on the notion of taking her to America. "But you'll have to come with me right away," I said, "tomorrow! I'll come and get you. Early in the morning. And you'll come with me, Stasinka!"

She went into the house. I knew she would come with me tomorrow. For she would obey. Then she would be in my grasp and I would watch her break in my power.

I came for her in the morning. She appeared hatless and with her possessions wrapped in a bundle. She walked to the train station a few paces behind me. I bought both of us first-class tickets. Let Stasinka see who I was. But she sat silently in her seat, her eyes unmoving.

In Hamburg I bought her a hat and a dress. She was neither surprised nor grateful. She acquiesced silently.

We boarded the ship; I traveled first class, she third class. Maybe she would understand better when she saw the difference. Every day I had her brought to my cabin and served a refreshment. She ate in silence, breathing heavily. Long after she had gone the smell of her body filled the cabin. I sat there inhaling it like the smoke of a cigar. I no longer wanted to possess her now. I only wanted to see Stasinka revolt against me, to hear her cry out. But she remained silent and her eyes gazed at me lusterless.

In New York we stayed at a small hotel. Stasinka got a little garret room. For myself I took a room on the second floor. Then I set about doing what had flashed through my mind when I stood before Stasinka in the hospice garden.

I knew where to meet the right people in New York; I went

to a small café frequented by Russian and Polish Jews. It was a tiny, smoke-blackened place with plush banquettes, once red, against the walls. The guests, many with their hats on, sat at little marble tables that stood crowded close together. Some of the guests moved from table to table or stood in the narrow aisles between the tables. The room was filled with the yells of the gesticulating people and the clatter of dishes being filled and washed in a corner of the room. A waiter, pale, with sleepy eyes and a greasy tailcoat, carried glasses of tea on a big tray.

I looked around for a seat. In one corner a man, a Galician Jew by the looks of him, sat alone at a table. I joined him. He scrutinized me for a while, then spoke.

"New to New York?" he said.

"New yourself," I said curtly.

He saw at once that I was no greenhorn. Slowly he stroked his sparse brown beard. His hand was delicate and fragile as a child's. His lashless, inflamed eyes wandered the room restlessly.

The light of a rainy day shone dully through the grimy windows. I gazed out impassively onto the street and waited for my neighbor to speak again.

After a pause he started up again:

"You're in business?"

"No. I steal things."

He smiled at my joke.

"Business, I figured. What's your racket, might I ask? I can tell you, there are ways to get together. Who knows, maybe we can get together too."

I gave my companion a penetrating look. Then I glanced

around cautiously, as if to make sure that no one was listening.

"Stuff and nonsense!" he said, accompanying the words with a scornful wave of his hand. "What do you need to be afraid of? My name is Seidenfeld. Stolen goods, then?"

"No one's stolen these goods yet," I said meaningfully. Now he gave me a penetrating look. I met it calmly.

"I see," said Seidenfeld, and again his elegant little hand stroked his beard, "I see. Young?"

"Maybe twenty-eight."

"Bit old. Could you say pretty?"

"You could say pretty. Fat."

"Fat? That's not the taste these days. Maybe at Beller's. Polacks go there. They like 'em fat. So we can try. Bring the gal here."

"Twenty dollars," I said. It came to me quite suddenly. I had to make money on it, if only one grubby dollar. I had to sell her. Sell her. And make a dollar on it. I smiled triumphantly at the thought.

"Twenty dollars!" Seidenfeld cried out as if in mortal anguish. "Twenty dollars, when they're running down your door these days, what?"

He drummed his fingers on the table. How is it possible, I thought, for this person to have such fragile little hands?

"What are you willing to pay, then?" I asked.

He turned his face to me full on. I saw that his eyes were not alike. The left eye was half-shut. In a grave tone, emphasized by an energetic gesture of his right hand, he said:

"First I have to see the kalleh!"

At that I burst out in hideous laughter, shuddering and coughing. I laughed and coughed at the same time. My childhood, my youth, my past burst out in this vicious laughter. The people in the café turned to stare at me. And Seidenfeld looked at me as if I'd gone crazy.

"Never heard of such a thing! Laughing, are you? Can you buy without seeing? Who ever bought without seeing? You ever bought before?"

"You're right," I said, still breathing with difficulty. I had to wipe the tears from my cheeks. "Something just occurred to me, Herr Seidenfeld. Of course you can see her."

I went straight away and got Stasinka. She sat at the table and we bargained over her in her presence. I kept looking at her out of the corner of my eye. Her breasts rose and fell. But otherwise she was like a mass of lifeless flesh.

Seidenfeld gave me five dollars. Then I brought Stasinka to Beller. We sat in the carriage and Seidenfeld sat on the coachbox. I jingled Seidenfeld's silver dollars in my pocket.

"Stasinka," I said. "You didn't want me. But I care for you, and so I'm giving you a thousand Silesian Polacks instead of me."

Once more, with all the savagery in me, I grabbed Stasinka by the breasts, the breasts I had seen before me all these years since my boyhood, rising, falling, big and heavy.

In the dark narrow side street housing Beller's establishment, I got out and walked away.

The next evening I visited the New World — that was the name of the house where I had taken Stasinka. When I rang, a grinning Negro opened the door and led me up the stairs. I heard the petrified music of a player piano from the salon and entered without taking off my coat.

The smell of sweat and strong drinks washed against me, worse than I remembered from my days as a bar-waiter. Sofas of every color stood against the walls, and little tables stood in the corners. The space in the middle was clear, probably for dancing. A wearily burning gas lamp immersed everything in a twilight which blurred all contours.

Several girls, about five of them, lounged about on the sofas. Stasinka sat in one corner dressed in a scrap of red silk which left her breasts almost completely exposed. She gazed dully at the floor.

I took a seat in the opposite corner. A Jewess with rotten black teeth came up to me. I ordered whisky. The sound of Stasinka's even breaths seemed to reach all the way to where I sat. For a moment I felt her eyes upon me. Then she looked straight ahead again.

Several men arrived with a ruckus, longshoremen by the looks of them. They sat at the next table. Mrs. Beller, a black-haired, gaunt woman with pitiless eyes, gave the girls a sign. They rose wearily and sat next to the men. Only Stasinka stayed where she was.

I would have liked to ask the girl at my table how Stasinka had acted when she came to the house. Whether she had cried, screamed, cursed or kept quiet. But I was afraid to show my interest in Stasinka openly.

"A new girl?" I asked, glancing toward the corner where Stasinka sat.

"A new girl," she said. She appeared to have witnessed events such as a "new girl's" initiation into a house so many times that it was not even worth her while to discuss it.

"She's quiet." I tried to keep up the conversation. But the girl just shrugged her shoulders as if to say: My God, everyone has their little quirks.

A big man at the next table rose and headed toward Stasinka. She sat motionless while he talked to her. I knew she would have sat motionless even if she had understood what the man was saying to her.

The woman joined them, her malignant eyes fixed sternly on Stasinka. Stasinka rose and went, swaying her hips as if carrying the heavy buckets to the well in the hospice garden. The man followed her.

Stasinka's head was bowed to the ground, and I felt she was saying:

"Those are the woman's orders."

I jumped to my feet and stared after Stasinka until she vanished behind the low door to her room. I stopped outside the door. The girl from my table came up to me and said something that went in one ear and out the other. She snuggled up against me. But I pushed her away and hurried off.

I had thought I would gloat after humiliating Stasinka so utterly. But I felt no gloating within me when I saw Stasinka vanish into her room in the New World. As I went down the stairs, past the grinning Negro, I felt as if I had left something half-done, as if I had to turn around and beat Stasinka to death. The dumbness of her lightless, heavy soul, dully obedient to all that I cruelly inflicted upon her, made me fear that for all my hatred I was defenseless against Stasinka the maid.

That evening in Beller's New World I saw Stasinka for the last time in my life. The next day I met a man who made me a deal. It struck me as a good thing, and I put my money into it. It was a speculation with a recently discovered oil well. The business took up so much of my time that I was unable to go see Stasinka. Fourteen days later I sold my share at a profit of twelve thousand dollars — fortunately for me, as it later turned out that the well did not exist.

Now I finally found the time to visit Beller's establishment. To my astonishment, Stasinka was no longer there.

I asked Beller about her. He was a fat blond man with tiny eyes, one fat cheek and one thin. His nose rose crookedly from his face. He told me she had found a job in a small town. And she'd probably fit in better there, too. He named a small town out west.

I did not doubt for a moment that I would have to travel in pursuit of Stasinka. She was no longer in the town Beller had named to me. Her trail led to a neighboring town, from there to another, once again without success. And so for about four weeks I sought Stasinka in vain. Then I gave up hope and went to Francisco.

In Francisco I was offered the opportunity to become a partner in a small stovepipe factory. I invested my money in it, laying the cornerstone of my present fortune. The factory flourished; every year we were able to expand it in one way or another. On top of this came lucky speculations and not least the persistence with which I undermined my partner's position until he was finally forced to accept a relatively small sum of money in compensation and leave the business to me.

Once a year I ran an announcement in the newspapers asking Stasinka to contact me. I never got a reply. Still, I was far from giving up hope of meeting her again. I felt that she owed me something, and that I had the right to demand that fate settle this debt.

I had power and gold and was master over many. Thousands labored for me in my factory, men, women, children. I was a hard and relentless master to all the people in my power. But Stasinka had escaped my power.

My firm belief that I would meet Stasinka again was to be disappointed. I did hear from her once more, but in a different way than I had expected.

I was sitting in my office when the servant announced a woman who refused to go away, even though I did not receive visitors at that hour. I had the woman shown in. She was about forty, common, dressed in a blue blouse which hung loosely over her skirt, plump, toothless. In her arms she carried a boy about two years old.

When I asked her what she wanted, she told me she was a midwife in a town near the coast. About two years ago one of her patients instructed her to raise the boy she had delivered and bring him to me once he was old enough to weather the hardships of the journey to Francisco. The woman had died in childbed of a high fever, and she, the midwife, was discharging her promise to the dying woman by bringing me the boy.

"The woman is dead?" I asked. There was no doubt in my mind that the boy was Stasinka's child.

The woman affirmed.

"You're lying!" I cried.

The woman took the death certificate from her pocket, along with several other documents to show me that I was not being swindled. Stasinka's employment book verifying her faithful services as a maid in the hospice, her ticket for the ship and the record of her work at Beller's.

There was no doubt about it. Stasinka was dead.

I took her death as nothing more or less than the defrauding of my right to master her one day; ever since my boyhood, ever since the days and nights in the hospice where my childhood had been confined, this wish had burned undimmed.

But Stasinka had fled life, fleeing me.

Now I stood there with power and gold, but Stasinka, for whose sake I had wanted power, was dead.

I rang for the servant.

"Take this woman to the cash office and have her paid two hundred dollars." My eye fell on the boy. "The child stays here."

The woman left. I went up to the boy, lying on the table. He shrank away from me and shrieked. He was afraid of me. I thought I saw Stasinka's dumb animal gaze again in his eyes. Kill him, I thought, kill him! I looked for an instrument. Paper scissors fell into my hands. I approached the child. Crying no longer, he stared at me fixedly.

I turned away. I had the servant bring the woman back.

"Do you have a month's time?" I asked. "I love this child. I want to provide for his upbringing. You will be handsomely paid," I said. Then I sat down and wrote this letter, addressed to the mayor of my hometown.

Dear Sir!

Chance has placed in my hands the fate of an unfortunate foundling, making me answerable before God, so to speak, for the future of this child, a two-year-old boy. I am unmarried, and would be compelled to entrust the child's upbringing to strangers. Myself raised by strangers, I can well imagine the development of a child deprived of the loving care which as a boy I was so fortunate to find in the hospice of your town. My time there laid the foundations which enabled me to hold my own in life and achieve the position of respect I now enjoy. The company of worthy old men taught me early on to appreciate the gravity of existence, and the portrait of the benefactor in the dining hall confronted me daily with a man who in wealth did not forget the poor.

Now I am unexpectedly given the opportunity to provide for a little boy and at the same time show my gratitude to my hometown for my happy childhood. This very day I shall remit you 30,000 (thirty thousand) dollars with the stipulation that they be used to establish an additional vacancy for boys in the hospice, the first beneficiary being the boy presented to you by the bearer of this letter. Otherwise, this bequest shall conform to all the stipulations of the orphanage statutes. I ask only that my picture also be displayed somewhere in the hall of the hospice. I shall send it today along with the money.

One more thought occurs to me as I bring this letter to a close.

I am a rich man. Would I have become what I am today had I not been raised to austerity and industry in my youth in the hospice? Should I now raise this boy, found by chance, in luxury and wealth, or should I not rather give him the same foundations I myself received? I barely know this child, yet already I love him. For that reason I wish him to enjoy, as I did, the good fortune of a simple childhood in the hospice of my hometown.

I finished the letter, sealed it and gave it to the woman. Then I supplied her with money and sent her to Europe with the boy. Slowly I resigned myself to the fact that Stasinka was dead. She had left me her boy. In him I could still overthrow dead Stasinka. In him I made my life repeat itself all over again. Let him suffer my youth. Stasinka was broken after death in her child.

Several weeks after the midwife's departure I received a letter from my hometown in which the mayor reminded me that it was he, then the trustee of the hospice, who had given me my send-off. He was pleased to learn as an old man how the boy from the hospice had risen in life, though he had never doubted it, as he had always held the conviction, now confirmed once again, that honesty and diligence lead to success. Then he thanked me at length for my noble bequest.

Years passed, years in which my work in the factory absorbed me completely. Everything else had ceased for me. Now I had no interest in the world but the expansion of my business. Power for its own sake. I remained relentless toward my workers. During a strike I hired coolies as strikebreakers. I have been one of the most-hated employers in Francisco ever since.

I turned fifty, imperious, proud of my life's work, but lonely. I had no friends and no wife. Instead, I had money and enemies.

It would lead too far afield, and depart from the actual point of this story, if I were to describe this period of my life in greater detail. Moreover, I think that what I have mentioned of it, in conjunction with what I have said about my development as a whole, will suffice to give a clear picture of me.

Sometimes the memory of Stasinka returned, and anger rose within me. Then I thought of the growing boy in whom I was conquering her after all.

And so I arrive at the turning point of my life.

I received a letter:

Esteemed Benefactor!

On the day when, heavy-hearted, I depart the house where through your kindness I had the good fortune to be raised, my heart irresistibly compels me to convey my thanks to you. In your kindness you gave an innocent child the opportunity to develop the faculty of his soul and to awaken and increase the goodness which fate planted in his breast.

Now I am leaving the hospice where I spent my sheltered youth and, with good people's assistance, will visit a teacher's college in the city. For like you, esteemed benefactor, I feel the urge to devote myself to innocent children to show my thanks to God for sending me, an innocent child, my benefactor, just as gratitude at your own fate must have moved you to rescue me. Only I lack the means to be grateful in the same way as you. And my modest aspirations are not toward riches, but to devote myself to goodness in quiet and simplicity. Thus I have decided to become a teacher, and I know that you will approve of this desire as well.

I assure you that your portrait has beheld no wickedness in my soul. At all times I felt your eyes, like those of the founder of my "paternal home," resting upon me, encouraging me to do what is right. With humble heart, content with the modest lot which providence has ordained for me, I leave the haunts of my youth, I leave the old men, to assist whom filled my heart with profound happiness.

Esteemed benefactor, I know you need no thanks. What you did for the foundling who does not know his parents, you did for his poor mother. In the child in whom, I know, the soul of the dead woman is repeated, you have brought happiness after death to the life of one who was surely unfortunate, who surely bore many a great burden and who, for she was my mother, no doubt bore them patiently. And you are richer for knowing: I have done a good deed!

You are not to know the name the hospice gave me, lest you feel called to support me financially. And do not inquire after it! I am satisfied with my lot and can think of no better.

The boy to whom you did good.

Letting the letter drift to the floor, I stared in front of me for a long time, dismayed by memories and the tone of the letter. I saw Stasinka's boy before me and heard him say: You've done a good deed.

A shrill bell roused me. Automatically I followed it into the factory. I walked down the long production halls in the narrow aisle between the rows of gleaming, eternally turning wheels. I heard the din of work as if from afar.

The director was waiting for me at the end of the last hall, where my factory's products were prepared for shipment. He showed me the latest model, just finished, and began to report on its merits, referring to his notes and to the apparatus which stood great and gleaming before us.

I heard his words without understanding them. In the middle of his report I turned and went.

In my office I reread the letter of the boy to whom I had done good. I surprised myself by feeling no anger. Didn't I want to do him ill? Didn't I want to make him suffer? And Stasinka in him? But the boy stood there before me and said: in me you brought my mother happiness after death.

And so the boy, like Stasinka, had escaped my power. Vividly, more vividly than she had in a long time, Stasinka stood before me and I saw her dumb submissive gaze: those are the woman's orders. And I experienced something that had not happened as long as I could remember. All at once tears ran down my cheeks.

I wept. My childhood woke once more, and I saw it pressed into one single image before my eyes. I saw the hospice and the poverty of my youth and saw hatred and loathing of poverty grow along with me. I saw myself as the factory-owner before whom the host of workers trembled, the workers I hated because they were poor and despised because they were without power. I saw Stasinka, hated, guiltless, who let my power run its course as if she did not feel it. I saw the boy I hated because he was a child, because he was at my mercy, because he had Stasinka's meek eyes, the boy I wanted to let suffer and make evil, just so that all the simplicity of the soul, all the dumbness of obedient hearts, his mother Stasinka within him, might laugh and soil itself, twisted into its opposite.

And now: childish hands reach for the roots of my soul and I weep at the kind embrace.

I wanted to deliver up a child to a fate like mine and let him grow up to become like . . . me, a man of power? Could that be the madness of hatred: what I wished to destroy, I wished to make like me? Did I guess, without realizing it, that my life, so rich in power, was poor and luckless because hatred made it lonely, because it was hemmed in by enemies, coldness, estrangement? And now I knew that my life too had cried out for warmth and kindness, for I could think of no worse and crueler way to hate and kill than to have Stasinka's child live my own life. But the child turned out humble and good. And his goodness calls out to me.

I wept at the hatred I had sown for destruction and whose end was transformed by fate.

Tears washed the hatred from my soul. I felt as if gentle light were shining within me.

In the light of this good love I saw Stasinka, the Lord's dumb creature. She was one of the obedient, the meek. But I was the element that invaded a life enclosed in God to destroy the nature of the humble, because hatred is enmity. But the good love was not destroyed and was stronger than evil. It speaks from the boy to me and answers him from within me.

Stasinka was killed. But after death happiness came to her.

Goodness and humility are so great that even the evil murderer's heart is touched by the ray of happiness.

I opened the window. Before me was Francisco, wheel-churned, crowd-packed, howling, snorting, raving. And in the west I saw the sea. But over Francisco and the greed and hatred of its people and over the sea and over a thousand cities filled with struggle and enmity there was a bridge from a poor boy to me.

I lean out of the window. I want to come closer, God, I want to come closer! — The street is loud. People drift side by side without seeing each other.

Somewhere, I think, there has been a murder. Stasinka has been killed again.

But I am no longer alone.

O, that one creature loves me . . .

STORY OF A MURDER

I do not know whether my aversion to hunchbacks arose from my deep aversion to the hunchbacked barber in our town or whether it was the other way around, that this man confirmed my original aversion to cripples. It seems to me that I have always felt an insurmountable loathing toward all whom God has marked with humps, ulcers, leprosy, eruptions and other such defects, indeed toward all things weak and frail, even toward animals, at least those not naturally furnished with vigor and strength.

From this one might suppose that I myself have always been a vigorous man bursting with health. Let me make it clear at the outset that just the opposite is true. I was so sickly that once I finally gained entrance to military school, by calling upon all my father's connections, I had to leave only half a year later. All my life I was short, slight, scrawny, my face was always pale as wax, my shoulders so high that I gave the impression of slight deformity. I had perpetual dark blue rings around my eyes, my joints and bones were fragile, and are to this day. Is it surprising that I hated all weak things just the same? Isn't it true, in fact, that there is nothing one can hate and despise so wholeheartedly as oneself or one's reflection?

I will tell the story of a deed which is the story of my youth. My boyhood was not embraced by love as others' are. No one was ever kind to me. Just once did a person speak to me as if to a person, if only in a letter. My judges showed no pity toward me, and even my lawyer called me hardened and depraved by the wretchedness of my circumstances, by heredity from a depraved father. The judges sentenced me to twenty years of penal servitude, the harshest sentence they could pass upon me at my age. I was seventeen years old at the time. Now I am thirty-one.

I am not unhappy in this house, nor am I impatient. I rejoice in the severity of my warders, I rejoice in the compulsive regularity of sleep, work and exercise to which I am subjected. I love this kind of life, and sometimes I feel that I am not a convict, but a soldier, the simple obedient soldier I wanted to become. I love to obey.

In six years I will leave this house. People who leave prison after years or decades of incarceration are not said, as a rule, to return as viable members of human society. Yet I believe I will not leave prison a broken man. I will cross the threshold of this house serenely, not to revel in a freedom long foregone. I will go into service, a trade. I have learned to work a lathe here, displaying such skill that even the director of the house has had me manufacture certain items for his own use. I hope to support myself with this skill when my time is served.

I said that I sometimes feel like a soldier here. Let me add that this word does not encompass quite, or all of, what I feel here. When I sit in my cell in the evening and look up at the tiny barred window, I often feel that I am not a convict, but a monk. A quiet obscure little monk, a simple monk whose Father

Superior is content with him, and I smile, and sometimes I fold my hands on my knees. No, there is no longing for the world in me, only patience, calm, contentment. If my judges, my lawyer and the women who watched my trial saw me like this, no doubt they would only repeat that I am a hardened, callous and depraved person. I sit there and smile. A murderer! And sit there and smile like a meek contented monk.

Am I really a murderer? I killed a man. But I seem not to have done it myself, so remote is the deed, so foreign to me. It is like a monastic castigation I inflicted once upon myself, not upon the murdered man. As if the scar were still upon my back. But healed. Even now I savor the memory of this castigation of the flesh and rejoice in it, for I have no instrument in my poor cell to punish afresh this body wasted by asceticism, to punish not from hatred, not from vengeance, not to drive out the pleasures of the senses, but from a feeling I cannot clearly describe: I call it obedience.

Yet I do not want to lose myself in contemplation of my present existence, but rather to tell the story of my life as briefly as I can. I was only seventeen years old when it happened, and I had seen and experienced little. Apart from my brief spell at the military school, I had never left the small town where my father and I moved several years after my birth, after his discharge and my mother's death. My father and I lived on the first floor of a narrow two-storied house next to the church at the lower end of the slightly sloping marketplace: this is where I grew up.

I remember my father as vividly as if he stood before me in

the flesh. Though his appearance had begun to deteriorate just before the incident, even then he retained the erect carriage of his torso, still wore his long, black, no longer immaculate jacket buttoned to the top. I know that despite our impoverished circumstances, which must have burdened my father greatly, he used to go to the barber first thing every day, where he had his chin clean-shaven, his sideburns trimmed and his moustache twirled.

In town he was never called anything but the General. At first this name was no doubt given to mock the old gentleman with the soldierly airs. Later my father's nickname caught on to such an extent that no one addressed him any other way, as if the title were my father's due. At first my father may have perceived it as ridicule, but noticing that people kept a straight face — perhaps only to laugh at him all the more heartily afterwards — he must have begun to feel flattered, and it is possible that in the end he himself believed in his rank. At any rate, he would have been deeply insulted if anyone had refused him the title. In reality my father never was a general, and could not have become one, as he had not even been an officer, but an army surgeon, and had left the service as a surgeon-major. He was forced to do so not by age or illness, but because he had been implicated in irregularities in the administration of the funds entrusted to him as the commander of a large military hospital. Aided by a relative of my mother, my father did manage to replace the missing sums and hush up the affair thoroughly enough to head off an inquiry. Nonetheless, he had no choice but to hand in his resignation.

My mother had been ailing for years, and all the excitement seems to have taken such a toll on her that she died. My father decided to leave the town where he had last served and move to the small town where he was born as the son of a civil servant. This move must have been prompted by the desire to flee the furor that his sudden resignation would inevitably cause, as well as the necessity of severely curtailing his living expenses. Not only was his pension small, every month he had to remit a considerable portion of it as an interim payment to the relative whose considerable loan had enabled him to put the funds back in order before handing them over.

In the narrow, dark house by the church we lived in an apartment consisting of a kitchen and two rooms. At first we kept a maid to do the chores and prepare our meals. But my father soon wearied of eating and passing the time in our dark, shabbily furnished rooms, and he began to take his meals in the inn. Consequently the maid was dismissed. Now a charwoman came every morning to make the beds, brush the clothes and polish the shoes. I was given my meals in the kitchen of the inn, while my father grew more and more accustomed to spending his time in the taproom. Home was a lonely place, the paint on the walls was old and cracked, dust lay in thick layers on trunks and cabinets; everything exuded such neglect that I too preferred to sit on the dark wooden stairs rather than in the apartment.

From earliest childhood I shunned all companionship. I did not walk home with my fellows when classes were over, and I never played with them. Because I made no secret of the fact that I wanted to be a soldier, an officer, they nicknamed me "the little soldier." I ignored their ragging, and my schoolmates called me proud. Only once did I let a schoolmate pick a fight with me, which I, the weakling, naturally lost, especially with all my other schoolmates siding against me. That was when one of the boys asked me with mocking laughter what I was so proud about, anyway, was it that my father had risen to the rank of general?

Was I proud? Now I know I was only unhappy. The stigma on my father, who had been so dishonorably stripped of his uniform and now, old and gray, played such a ludicrous role in the town, repelled me from everything, filling me with deep bitterness and making me lonely. I loved this old man who blundered into lower and lower depths and whose dignified demeanor, soliciting awe of his rank, made him all the more ludicrous the lower he sank. I do not know whether he ever realized the effect he had on people, whether he guessed that they did not believe his pose and his stories, whether he knew that they were secretly smirking at him when they swept off their hats and addressed him as "Herr General," or whether he saw through it all and shouldered the painful tragedy of a destiny behind whose mask alone, perhaps, life was still possible for him. I do not know. I feel that he feared me, the only one who saw through him completely. With horror I recall — and these are among the most painful memories of my childhood — those rare times when I was alone with my father. Usually I was asleep, or pretended to be asleep, when he came home late at night, walking unsteadily, treading with anxious care lest he wake me. But sometimes, when the torment of his gout confined him to the house, we sat together. His eyes hid from mine. Ordinarily the tireless storyteller, he said not a word. The dignity had fled from his face, which conveyed only fright and helpless uncertainty. It was as if his heart were filled with the terrible fear that I, who knew all, might open my mouth and speak. If he was speaking with someone on the street in his resounding voice, and I, his son, drew near, he would fall silent and look shyly at the ground. And all the while I felt that my father's shyness of me was turning into enmity toward me as his initiate, not because I was privy to the reasons for his resignation — the whole town knew them — but because I was the only person in whose eyes he saw the knowledge of how little he, the "General" himself, believed in the sorry role he played so proudly and so entertainingly. Later, when my father may actually have come to live the game that had been forced on him, when, barely sober now, he took the martyrdom of a once-conscious sham for reality, he was my enemy and stayed that way. His shyness of me vanished then, but with it went the barrier that had stood in the way of his enmity, and he hardened toward me and did not spare me.

I believe the hunchbacked barber Josef Haschek was much to blame for this change in my father's attitude. Whenever I think back on this time of my life, on the whole period before the crime, the figure of Josef Haschek looms before me, and no doubt that is why, unpracticed in the written description of events, I took that man as my starting point when I began writing this account. That ugly, hunchbacked man with his long arms hanging almost to his knees is like a symbol to me of that ugly, lonely and unhappy time.

Josef Haschek's torso was shaped like a cube standing on one point and somewhat flattened at the top. One corner of this cube projected far out from his chest and one from his back. His head, which rocked back and forth very oddly when he walked, rested between his shoulders without a neck. I am reminded of a clock we children marveled at in the window of a watchmaker's shop on the marketplace. It was a pendulum clock crowned by a moor's head with movable eyes. This head must have been connected to the pendulum, which set it in regular motion. It had no neck either; its chin barely peeked out, a circumstance which lent the movements of this head something I find horridly comical, making me recall it when describing the barber's rocking head.

I do not know how the barber Haschek managed first to win my father's trust, then gain more and more influence over him and at last dominate him completely. Haschek was one of the chief witnesses at my trial, and it is largely due to him that my judges hardened their hearts against me and regarded me as a creature incapable of moral feeling. He told them all that could make me abhorrent in the eyes of those who were to judge me, and he achieved his goal. He was my enemy as long as I can remember.

I told how I have always loathed all that is weak, diseased and sickly. It may be that the barber dimly sensed my aversion and this is what first stirred his hatred against me. Also, he may have noticed my silent disapproval as an increasingly cordial friendship developed between him and my father. Certainly he, like all the others, construed my silence and my defiant aloofness, these fruits of my unhappiness, as pride, and it may have vexed this ugly man that I did not sit down with him to talk and listen to his chatter. Perhaps he sensed that I regarded my father's association with him as his deepest humiliation. For such people are like murderers on the run, taking fright at the sound of a dry leaf falling from a tree. Such people, I say, and I fear I will be misunderstood. For all I have said so far is that the barber was hunchbacked, weak and ugly, and that his head rocked strangely between his shoulders when he walked.

Such people are violent, domineering, merciless and cruel toward all weaker things that come into their power. Such people, such ugly, deformed, weak people are obsequious and humble toward all who are stronger than they. But they hate them and are capable of destroying them if they show a weakness or fall into their hands. Such people are shrewd. They are shrewder than the strong, healthy, straight of limb. They laugh at the placidity of the healthy that comes from good digestion, inwardly they mock their erect gait, their dignified stride, product of their mediocrity. But shrewdness does not lift such people above the mediocre, the healthy. Their laughter is not insightful irony, it is a wounding weapon whose edge turns inward and painfully goads their own flesh. Such people live under pressure of a chronic fear, like criminals on the lam, for even if they have committed no crime, everything in them is ready to do so at any moment. Such people perpetually suspect one of despising them, thinking them ugly, sneering at their ugliness, being sickened by them. They are vainer than the good-looking. They love to dress flamboyantly, even to sport a flower in their buttonhole, as if insolently provoking mockery, perhaps because it torments them to display their wretched, wasted body to all eyes, the body which they themselves hate and despise more than others despise it, more than they themselves hate and despise anything in the world.

Perhaps the barber was my particular enemy because in truth I was his kin, and yet different from him. For I had not yet given myself up. He had already succumbed to the knowledge of his weakness and sickliness, if indeed he had ever resisted it. But I was governed by the thought of a goal that did not leave me until I committed the deed, and so I was not yet defeated. Perhaps it was the certitude of this thought which gave my unhappiness the appearance of pride and made me solitary. My solitude made the barber my enemy, not only because he hated solitary people, but because I was like him and solitary all the same. For people of his kind are not solitary. They want people to listen to them, to watch them bare themselves, violate themselves in words, in laughter, tears and gestures, from the hankering to chafe their own wretchedness and keep alive the thought of avenging themselves upon their listeners.

Oh God, oh God! Believing myself to be describing the barber, it seems to me I have also described myself as I was then. All I have said he had in him, oh God, I had it in me as well. I, too, was small and weak, pale, sickly, and ugly like all sick things; one might have thought me deformed, even if I had no hump. Wasn't I also violent and cruel toward all weaker things that fell into my hands? Later I will tell how I tortured animals. Wasn't I obsequious and humble toward the strong man, even as I hated him? How else could I have kept silent when the stranger humiliated me — hated him, envied him and kept silent? But when he fell into my hands — only now do I realize how I became the instrument of revenge against him, the ugly worm's revenge upon the giant! No, no, now I feel that this did not simply lie in the chain of happenstance. That I did so because, so born, I had to do so. In me, too, was the uncertainty and unrest of constant fear, as if each hour could bring me a humiliation so complete that I would not have the strength to survive that hour, unmasking me, revealing me, exposing me to full view, disclosing my lie, my crime. I, too, a criminal on the run. And have yet to lie, yet to trespass. Yet! But the crime is on its way. Oh God, now, fourteen years a convict, I realize only now that all that happened was no accident. Didn't I suspect that I was despised? And was it not that, in fact, which gave me my goal? Was I not vain? While the barber adorned his jacket with a flower, for what reason, if not vanity, did I still wear my snug, bright uniform jacket with yellow braid and buttons long after I had left the military school? And didn't I loathe the barber for the same reason he was my enemy, because we recognized ourselves in each other?

I do not know who will read this account one day. Perhaps he will not understand what I want to say, and find much to be contradictory. But it seems to me that all contradictions are merely apparent. One must remember that nothing that comes from us grows from a single root.

Once the barber had gained my father's trust, he used it to cast me from his heart. It is thanks to him, I believe, that for a long time I had to take my meals in the kitchen of the inn with servants and beggars, that my father lost all trust in me and beat me harder and more often the lower he sank and the more often he got drunk. In court Haschek claimed that the reason for my father's friendship with him was the old man's barely fathomable interest in the barber's niece, Milada, who kept house and helped out in the barbershop. And he claimed Milada's child was the child of the General, who despite his age — as the barber had often had occasion to observe — was still in full possession of his powers. The barber would have elaborated upon these observations, but the presiding judge silenced him. Milada herself refused to testify on this point. Ashamed to tell the truth, she let the lie stand. For the hunchback had lied. I know it. For I saw everything.

After my return from the military school I was apprenticed to Haschek, despite my staunch resistance. I experienced this as the deepest humiliation that could be inflicted upon me. The profession alone repelled me. It always cost me an inner struggle to lean over a man's bristly face and soften the skin with white lather. Later, when I wielded the razor myself, I often felt tempted while scraping the stubble to cut into the skin and make the red blood trickle down the lathered cheeks. On top of that, I had to learn the profession from the hunchbacked barber. I shall not describe the suffering I endured at Haschek's hands during my apprenticeship, when he beat me and forced me to perform services of the basest kind. I shall mention only that every morning when I arrived at the barbershop I first had to go to the room in the back where the barber slept, drag Haschek's chamber pot out from under the bed and empty it into the privy. The hunchback would never forgo the pleasure of watching my every move as I performed this task. Even today, here in my cell, the room's revolting smell of greasy pomades and tinctures rises in my nostrils. My consolation was that this time would pass and one day I would be a soldier after all.

I knew that the hunchback was lying, but in court I said nothing at first. For I felt that such disputes would only soil my father's memory still further. After the verdict was pronounced, and the trial already over, I said quietly, but in the silence all around the words were clearly audible: "My father was not the father of the child." Seeing that everyone was staring at me uncomprehending, no doubt because they had all forgotten this unimportant episode of the trial, already a day in the past, I repeated it more clearly: "The General was not the father of Milada's child." Then I was taken away.

The father of Milada's child was Milada's uncle, the hunchback. Milada was the orphaned daughter of Haschek's sister. She was tall, slender, with blonde hair and small but well-formed breasts. When I entered the barber's service she was about twenty-five years old and had been in the house for a year. She was not old, but her face was faded, no doubt from the poverty and privations she had endured earlier on. Soon after I entered Haschek's service I noticed that something was going on between the two of them, though neither the barber nor Milada ever breathed a word of it. I could tell from Milada's reddened eyes and because I sometimes found her crying. I saw that she also suffered at the hands of the hunchback, who had her in his power because he could turn her out of the house again without a penny at any time. I saw that she struggled against him and that she grew quieter, humbler and more submissive by the day. She succumbed. But before she succumbed she was also to be disappointed in me.

Perhaps Milada would not have succumbed had it not been for this disappointment. Perhaps before this disappointment she had held out hope, and only surrendered once she saw that she was utterly alone: so perhaps I, too, am to blame.

One day when the barber had gone I found Milada sitting in the dark hallway between the two living chambers and the barbershop. She was crying. I no longer know what moved me to go up to her and ask her what had happened. Milada lifted her face and looked at me for a minute. At that moment she may have seen me as her companion in adversity, the ally who suffered at the same person's hands. I bent down to her. But she stretched out her arms to me, sobbing, flung them around me and hugged me to her. At that I broke free, pushed Milada away so roughly that she almost fell, and ran away.

It may be that when she drew me toward her the hateful smell of pomade which clung to Milada as to everything, every piece of furniture, every implement at Haschek's, to me, rose up and repelled me. It may be — I was never consciously aware of it — that I could not ally myself with her, healthy and straight of limb, against the hunchback, even if he was my enemy. That I took the disgust, the revulsion she felt toward the hunchback as disgust toward me as well, even if, in this moment of need, she embraced me as the lesser and more harmless evil, perhaps in a more sisterly than womanly embrace. But there may be a different reason for my behavior toward Milada: that is, my attitude toward women has always been one of cool disapproval. However, I was still young at the time, and since then, since my seventeenth year, I have had no further opportunity to test this attitude of mine. Yet never in all the years of my sentence has it even occurred to me to desire such a test. I have heard that boys of the age I was then, that men, even, dream of women and sexual orgies. Never have I seen any of that in my dreams.

Soon after betraying Milada I grew aware of a change in her which, inexperienced though I was at the time, I grasped at once. She seemed fully reconciled with the hunchback; it was as if she had overcome her disgust. She joked with him, acted cheerful, and no one who saw her now would have thought that only a few days ago she had moved about these rooms like a humble, fearful servant. There was another thing I noticed, and here, too, the reasons were immediately clear to me. Now Milada, who had so far been friendly toward me, also began to persecute me with her enmity; she complained to the hunchback about my laziness, my disobedience, she approved when he beat me, even goaded him on, and thought up ways of her own to wound and torment me. I had to empty and clean her chamber pot too, which, unlike other healthy people, she used for all her needs. I understood her. I had thrust her away and left her at the hunchback's mercy. It was my fault. She had overcome her revulsion of him, but perhaps only by finding me to shift her hatred to.

Twice already I have tried to convey what I consider the

reason for the strange relationship which developed between the barber and my father, and both times it was my inexperience in storytelling that made me stray from the straight line of the account. But now I will set about amending the oversight.

When my father, as an army surgeon sent packing, returned to the town he had not seen since youth, he had no friends here whatsoever. The first acquaintance he made in town was the hunchbacked barber. My father made it a habit to lavish great care on his external appearance, as is customary in the city and especially in military circles, and to visit the barbershop as the first order of the day. Though my father no longer wore his uniform, nor did he now travel in circles which called for particular fastidiousness, he did not stop taking care of his appearance until the time just before the incident, and only then could one observe signs of neglect. My father must have visited Haschek's barbershop the very day of his arrival, and then repeated this visit daily. Even then people were beginning to call my father the General, though not yet openly. But the rumor must have already reached him. Josef Haschek was the first to address him directly by this title. It will seem incomprehensible that such a form of address, which at the time the old, long-suffering man had to take as rank mockery, could become the start of a friendship. I was not there, but I seem to see the hunchback standing before the gray-haired old man and positioning the razor to begin shaving the stubble on the sideburn-framed chin. And suddenly he says it, affixing it to some question, such as whether my father had slept well. "Herr General." My father looks up and sees the humble, dog-like devotion in this wretched man's eyes, gazing at him as if nothing had occurred but what anyone would have expected. At that moment, the great decision is made. Should my father stand up and cast this dwarf to the ground with a single blow? Should he at least adamantly refuse to be addressed by a title which is not his due? The man seems to believe what he is saying, and already he is speaking innocently of something else. And my father hesitates, wondering whether to disabuse him; then perhaps he remembers that waiters and barbers are in the habit of arbitrarily enacting elevations in rank and caste, addressing commoners as barons, students as doctors, perhaps even pensioned military men as generals. Once more, perhaps, he reassures himself that there is no mockery in the eyes and no mockery in the voice. Then my father is silent, and with this silence he has taken everything upon himself.

In the first years of their relations Josef Haschek would never have sat at the General's table when he happened to be at the inn in the evening at the same time as my father. My father was in the habit of sitting alone at a corner table, sometimes, later on, at the civil servants' table. Not until the taproom was deserted would the hunchback slink out of his corner, holding his beer glass, take up his pose and in a military tone ask "respectfully" for permission to take a seat at his table, at which my father smiled graciously and condescended to make an inviting gesture with his hand. Up to the very last, that is, when my father was virtually under the barber's control, the barber never forgot to assume the attitude of the subordinate soldier when speaking with my father. He always requested and reported respectfully, flung open the doors through which my father was about to step, and did not take a seat unless asked. All the while his face was grave and full of dignity; never could one have detected a smile of mockery. I believe the hunchback's behavior gave my father a sense of security and that the gravity of this game, over the years, gradually made my father believe in the reality of what at first he must have reluctantly endured. And it was the barber who brought him from silent toleration of the lie to speech. He forced him to lie. When they sat together by themselves in the inn, he pressed my father doggedly, albeit modestly, to share the treasure trove of his soldierly experience, to tell his adventures from the campaigns, especially as he, the hunchback, had already heard so much from others about my father's prowess and bravery and as he, who had no greater interest, indeed love, for anything than for the military, longed to hear of it from my father's lips. It is true that my father had taken part in campaigns, those against Denmark and against Prussia, but as a surgeon. Yet the barber wanted to hear how he had led the troops in a charge.

One can assume that my father did not yield to the barber's pleas at first. That only his relentless advances moved him to speak. That he hoped thereby to gain some respite. Perhaps, too, at some point the alcohol loosened his tongue. But if he had hoped the hunchback would be satisfied with one story, he was deceived. Haschek immediately spread the stories my father had told him, so that the very next evening, to amuse themselves with his lies, all the guests at the inn pressed my father to tell them of his deeds and adventures as well. What could my father do but continue down the path once taken? He was not strong enough to struggle against his fate, not wise enough to let his spirit rise in cool irony above the baseness of his fate and the baseness all around him, nor great enough of spirit to patiently shoulder the Passions of this road to Calvary, to humbly find in them peace and the reconciliation of the heart. And in this light his unhappy proclivity for drink, which made him sink still lower, but also let him forget, acquires the aura of a benevolent compensation by providence. At the time, I saw only his inebriation and his humiliation before others. These things filled my heart with bitterness. For only now do I know that they were all that kept my father from grasping the full magnitude of his ordeal.

Now, one might imagine that the hunchbacked barber did not do this to my father out of malevolence. One might imagine that he really approached him in sincere veneration. Oh, one must not forget that such people can have no veneration for my father's kind. My father was tall and proud, he saw to the cleanliness of his appearance, carried himself like a soldier whose chest is puffed out and whose thighs are accustomed to guiding a horse. He spoke curtly, loudly, and in a tone of command. Was the barber not compelled to be his enemy? My father was certainly not very clever, certainly nowhere near as clever as the barber. And yet he was a big man, despite the unfortunate story behind his retirement, proud, he spoke loudly and in a tone of command. They say the hunchback displayed not the slightest trace of a smile when he spoke with him. They forget the cleverness such people have. He knew he would lose his victim if even the shadow of a smile crossed his face. Such people's cleverness is ascetic. They do not smile, but their soul wallows in the consciousness of the mockery they inflict.

My youth was impoverished. And yet it, too, was lit by a light: the thought of my goal. I wanted to become a soldier. Perhaps somewhere, unbeknownst to me, my pitiful boy's body harbored the hope that once I had achieved my goal I would be big, healthy and strong like all soldiers. Perhaps it was this hope which made an essentially simple notion assume such extraordinary importance for me.

But above all I told myself that I must become a soldier because it was my duty to vindicate my father. Not by proving that he had been wronged. I never doubted his guilt. I wanted to vindicate him with a life of obedience, loyalty, the utmost fulfillment of duty in the very profession in which he had sinned. With my life I wanted to cleanse both him and me not only of his lapses in service but also of the subsequent disgrace into which he inexorably sank deeper and deeper. In a corner of our dark stairwell I wept at the thought of my father and my decision to atone for his sins. I wanted to be a soldier not only because my father had belonged to the caste as a surgeon, I was also drawn to the profession by its harshness and rigor. For I felt that only the most unsparing service, the grueling hardships and the pain of wounds, the obedience binding and absolute unto death, could liberate me from the disgrace and the stigma which my father had brought upon himself and me.

I had no illusions about my physical aptitude. But that knowledge did not prevent my will from fixing itself upon this goal. I know the stories of many commanders-in-chief; there were three whom I admired most of all and regarded as the greatest of soldiers. They were the Prince of Savoy, King Frederick the Second of Prussia and Emperor Napoleon Bonaparte: the hunchbacked little Prince Eugene, whose services had been turned down by a king of France; Frederick the Great, the gaunt, ugly man whose body, propped by a walking-stick, gave the impression of deformity as mine did; Napoleon, who was short and fat and made people laugh to see him clinging to the back of his horse! I believe to this day that a hump, however big, is no obstacle to a career as a commander. To be a truly great commander takes cruelty, the cruelty of deciding over the lives of many. The great commander has no mercy. No mercy toward himself either. I believe one must be deformed, disfigured by a malignant birthmark, to fully grasp the power placed in one's hands.

When I had completed the fourth form I set about putting my plans into effect. I wrote to the relative of my deceased mother who had once helped my father, and asked him to use his influence to help me get into military school and give me the chance at a career with few costs involved. With prodding and pleas I convinced my father to write to several old comrades asking them to back my petition for a scholarship, and especially to give me a letter for the military surgeon who would ascertain my fitness. I believe it was solely due to this letter from my father that I was declared fit.

My time at the military school was the only happy time of my youth. I served with passionate dedication, by no means drawn more to the theoretical subjects than to the physical exercises. On the contrary: it was my chief ambition to vie with my biggest and strongest comrades in drills and athletics, and I would sooner have collapsed unconscious than admit my exhaustion to a soul. It did not take much to exhaust me. Yet I clenched my teeth and mastered myself. I rejoiced when the officer gave me a direct order. Of course the atmosphere of obedience was all-pervasive. But only then, when the eyes of my senior officer rested on me and I stood there motionless, ready to comply with his order, did I feel penetrated, at once tormented and inspired, by the great desire of obeying. Perhaps one who desires dominion is inwardly full ready for the deepest humiliation of obedience when he finds the power that is stronger than he — indeed, perhaps his life is nothing but an agonized search for this power.

My military career soon came to an end. I had been at the military school only a few months when I collapsed unconscious after a long march and had to be taken to the infirmary, where I lay for some time with a high fever. From the infirmary I did not return to school, but was sent back home, where after stubborn but vain resistance I was apprenticed to the barber Haschek. Nevertheless, I did not give up the thought of a military career. I reckoned that once I had reached the requisite age I could enlist as a common soldier. And I hoped that I would manage through bravery and fulfillment of duty to climb the ladder of rank, even as a foot soldier.

Though for now I was nothing but a discharged cadet and barber's apprentice, I went on wearing my snug military jacket, as if to provoke people's scorn, perhaps because the rancor which their mockery stirred in me brought me one joy after all, the joy of letting it kindle my will over and over again.

I had been apprenticed in Haschek's barbershop for about a year when the stranger came to our town. I call him the stranger because no one in town called him anything else, and because all the witnesses called him that at the trial. I myself learned his name belatedly, long after the incident, in the course of the investigation. The arrival of the stranger, who appeared to be settling in for a long stay in our midst, created a great stir in the town, where travelers seldom strayed even for a few hours. He was discussed long and heatedly in the inn and by the customers in our barbershop, with avid speculation as to what business could have brought him to this town far from the beaten track.

The stranger had taken up lodgings in the inn on the marketplace, diagonally opposite the house where I lived with my father, the same inn whose taproom my father frequented. Asked by the curious innkeeper about the purpose of his stay, he responded evasively, saying only that he planned to stay in town for some time. I have no cause to explain what I believe induced the stranger to come to our town, especially as the reason is only loosely related to the incident and as I do not feel I have the right to reveal others' secrets. And so I will disclose only as much of the stranger's secret as is absolutely intrinsic to the understanding of my own story, on no account naming innocent persons by name and exposing their affairs to public scrutiny. However great the temptation, I will resist it in this account just as I resisted it during the investigation and the court hearing, though at the time it could have been to my advantage to communicate all the particulars.

The stranger visited the barbershop the very morning of his arrival. He was not dressed like the townsmen; the cut of his well-fitting suit bespoke the city man who selects his clothing with great care. The stranger's hair was black with a metallic sheen, cut short on the sides and parted in the middle. His moustache was short, and he had neither beard nor sideburns. The stranger was tall and slender of build, his movements were calm, slightly indolent like his gait, and perhaps it was this indolent calm in everything that gave the impression of a healthy, handsome body evenly developed in all its muscles. I had already seen the stranger earlier, when I left the house and crossed the marketplace to the barbershop. The carriage he sat in was just halting in front of the inn. I stopped, but the stranger did not rise at once, as I and others would have done upon arriving, to get out of the carriage. First he looked around for a moment. Then he slowly began to remove the lap robe tucked carefully around his feet and gave it to the coachman, who meanwhile had descended from the box. Only now did he rise and step out of the carriage.

All this is still quite clear in my mind. In particular I recall the care and weighty calm with which the stranger removed the lap robe from his feet. I also recall that the stranger's appearance, his calm and his confident indolence filled me with disapproval toward him, a feeling that solidified as I saw the mocking smile on the stranger's lips when I caught his eye in the barbershop, wearing my military jacket.

The stranger was tended to by Haschek, who tried vainly and tirelessly to engage the taciturn guest in conversation. The stranger gave short, evasive replies. I don't know whether he was simply not in the habit of speaking with barbers more than absolutely necessary, or whether he had decided for other reasons to avoid conversation so as to divulge no clues about the purpose of his stay.

I stood not far from Haschek and the stranger, sharpening razors on the razor-strop. As the hunchback ran the razor over his face I heard the stranger, no doubt feeling that Haschek had cut him in the cheek, cry "Stop," raising his hand as if in self-defense. At that moment an understanding smile crossed the barber's face:

"Respectfully beg your pardon," he said, "no harm done."

And lifting the razor again, he went on: "I thought it right off. I've served so many of the military gentlemen in my day. Even if I never saw action myself. Because . . . You can see for yourself, sir. Now, don't say a word, sir, beg respectfully. The gentleman is an officer. I know how to . . ."

He was about to go on, but the stranger interrupted him:

"I ask that you leave me in peace."

"Beg respectfully."

Haschek bowed and smiled.

I don't know whether Haschek really took the stranger for an officer or whether he only hoped to learn the truth from the unfamiliar guest this way. At any rate, when my father came in, soon after the stranger had left the barbershop, Haschek pretended that the stranger had conversed with him at length and divulged, albeit under the pledge of strictest secrecy, that he was an officer. What reasons moved the stranger to hide his rank, why he was planning to spend his time here, that the barber had not yet learned, mainly because he hadn't asked. He'd thought it unseemly to molest the stranger at their very first encounter with questions suggesting obtrusive curiosity, and thus he had learned only what the stranger had volunteered unasked. But there would surely be occasion to learn everything worth knowing, for the relationship of trust between him, the hunchback, and the strange officer, so gratifyingly evident at their very first meeting, would presumably continue to develop apace.

The barber's announcement seemed to make a profound impression upon my father. Though even then my father had probably sunk so low that he no longer felt the sadness and absurdity of his charade, a vague yet oppressive sense of guilt must have lingered within him, expressed mainly in a mistrust which grew by the day. I noticed that my father would start when a door was opened, only to smile as if released when he saw an acquaintance come in. It was as if he feared discovery, a surprise, any change, although he was probably no longer conscious of the charade that revolved around him. Certainly he had a mysterious shyness of strangers. He approached them only if there was no other choice and with a kind of sly, anxious caution — only to play his role all the more madly and uninhibitedly, in a triumphant mood, so to speak, once he felt that they had not come to throw his soul out of kilter. The notion that the stranger now threatening to enter the circle of his life was an officer must have made him, the General, especially insecure, filling him with amorphous fears.

When the barber had finished reporting his discussion with the stranger, my father looked at him fearfully and said in a toneless voice:

"An officer? An officer?"

"Yes, sir, Herr General!"

"Did he . . . Did you speak of me?"

"Yes, sir, Herr General. Naturally I mentioned the presence of an outstanding general in our town."

My father took a step toward the barber. His face, his form bespoke helplessness.

"Does he know me, Haschek?! . . . Does he know me?"

I believe this was when the hunchback conceived the idea that was to cause such calamity.

"Herr General, I respectfully report, he appears to have heard of Herr General."

"Did he say so, Haschek? Did he say it like that?"

"When I told him about Herr General, he said: 'Is that so!' As if to say: You think you have news for me, don't you, but I know much more about it than you do."

"He said 'Is that so,' Haschek? Was that all?"

"That was all. I respectfully beg you to take a seat, Herr General."

That evening at the inn I took my place at a table not far from the kitchen door. My father sat in a circle of burghers and civil servants at the opposite end of the taproom. The barber stood next to the table, joining in the conversation. My father was particularly expansive that evening. He told the story of a battle near a village whose Italian-sounding name I have forgotten. I don't believe that the war stories my father told were complete fabrications, but rather that he had heard them in the course of his service from officers who had actually experienced them. I doubt that my father had the imagination and inventiveness to make up such tales. All that he contributed were the often brazen embellishments of the story and the interpolation of his own person as the hero of the given military adventure. The barber listened to him with the closest of attention, and seemed to enjoy discovering minor inaccuracies in the story, pursuing contradictions by interposing questions and, when my father was at his wit's end, often answering them himself.

When I came in, my father was already in the middle of his story.

"So we're hunkered down quietly and starting to think: tonight it'll pass us by. The day before it cost us twenty-five dead and thirty-seven wounded to storm the graveyard. All the same, twenty-five dead. Some of the wounded were in such bad shape, whole feet gone, torn off just like that. Gentlemen! Bled to death in my hands!"

"Whose?" asked the barber.

"Bled to death in my hands, I say."

"The Herr General's? Where on earth was the surgeon?" asked the barber. "The coward must have . . . !"

My father lost his temper.

"Coward? Who's the coward? Always in the thick of things! I never deserted the wounded!"

"Herr General!" the barber said emphatically.

My father seemed to sense that he had said something

wrong, even if he did not know what. He looked at the barber, uncomprehending, abashed, and at a loss. Then he slumped as if overcome by an immense fatigue and said absently:

"Yes, yes!"

"Herr General," the barber said again, "I respectfully ask permission to make an incidental remark. I've heard it said that on all campaigns Herr General was so great a friend to the soldiers who had the honor of marching against the enemy under Herr General's command, that Herr General often deigned to take a hand himself in binding the wounds when haste was called for."

My father sat up straight again.

"Gentlemen, that's how it was. Took a hand myself in binding the wounds. Myself. Well, where was I?"

"You were hunkered down in a hollow. The day before you'd stormed the graveyard with great losses. You thought it would pass you by that night."

"We thought wrong, gentlemen, wrong! We're in the hollow. The village in front of us, and to the left and right skirmishers' fire. For cover, I dispatch a strong patrol, an officers' patrol, gentlemen, to move against the outskirts of the village. Always have to be cautious, gentlemen. I warn them not to be careless, however tired they are. I've seen cases where entire armies were destroyed by a detachment of a hundred cavalry led by a plucky officer, all because of a lack of cover. 'Pon my honor, gentlemen! Caution is a leader's greatest virtue. After cold-bloodedness and bravery, of course. Report from the patrol: village outskirts not occupied by the enemy. At that I order the patrol to disperse, disperse, that's important, gentlemen, advance toward the center of the village and hold their position until dawn, report any incidents, march in at dawn. I think to myself: now commend your soul to God, haven't slept for seventeen nights, good night! Oho! Comes a report from the colonel. My friend Colonel Kopal, gentlemen! My friend and commanding officer. Played billiards with him every day as a lieutenant in Temesvar, a kreuzer for ten points. Meet him in fifty-five as a captain in Mantua. Old warhorse. Ah, well; report: Colonel Kopal sick with a stomachache. I'm to take command of the battalion. Asks me to visit if things quiet down. What do I reply: Herr Colonel, I've taken command of the riflemen's battalion. I'll leave my battalion as a dead man, but not to pay a sick call. Colonel Kopal reads the message and bursts into tears. 'A soldier,' he cries, gentlemen, 'the very model of a soldier! God preserve him for our army!' "

"Herr General," said the barber, "I respectfully beg permission to interrupt Herr General. I had heard, you see, that Herr General served in the Italian campaign in the Alt-Starhemberg Regiment!"

"Yes indeed," my father replied, "in the time-honored Alt-Starhemberg Regiment whose colors I had the privilege as a young officer to bear in battles, skirmishes and assaults and to shield with my body. I tied it around my body and swam across the Po when it was flooded so you couldn't see the banks. And I rescued it, gentlemen!"

"I respectfully beg pardon," the barber said again, "I don't understand . . ."

He broke off and bowed deferentially. The stranger had entered and acknowledged the hunchback's salutation with a brief nod. He sat at the corner table farthest from the table where the group gathered around my father and farthest from my table as well, and ordered his dinner, which was brought to him at once. At my father's table conversation had ceased; everyone eyed the stranger curiously. My father cowered there as if to hide from the stranger behind the others' backs. But the stranger paid no attention whatsoever to the guests in the taproom. Only once did he look up and direct his scrutiny at my father's table for a moment, when the barber said, "That's what I don't understand, Herr General!" raising his voice to lend particular emphasis to the title he gave my father.

But my father, seeming to slump still further, said nothing.

The stranger ate quickly, rose and left the room. Once again the barber saluted him humbly. I got up and left as well.

Certainly there are many people in the world, and certainly many old soldiers, and surely writers have depicted them often enough and better than I am able, people who satisfy a mysterious desire by astonishing their fellows with the fabrication of untrue tales in whose truth they brook no doubt and which they themselves desire to believe absolutely. I do not know what causes this desire, be it alcohol or a morbid disposition, and I lack the knowledge and experience to get to the bottom of the phenomenon. But I do not believe my father is quite in a class with those characters often depicted in novels and plays, one or more of whom everyone has surely had ample opportunity to meet in real life. I would call these people "voluntary liars," for nothing but their own pleasure impels them to concoct their lies, and my father an involuntary liar, a liar from weakness, a liar from shame, not suited, like them, to cut a jolly figure in a comedy, but rather a pathetic one in a tragedy. My father stumbled into the snares the hunchback cunningly laid at his feet. He saw no way out, no way to find peace but in lies, and he gave himself up to them, unwillingly and reluctantly and with shame in his heart. I believe that this shame, however he sought to drown it in alcohol, still burned in his heart even after he had utterly lost himself in his lie, that the fear of meeting strangers was nothing but that same shame, joining with his vague sense of guilt to make him shy away from revealing his disgrace to a new person.

You will ask how it came that I, already so well aware of the predicament in which my father was entangled, did not go and snatch him from his fate. Why I did not expose the hunchback as a liar when he described his spurious conversation with the stranger. Why, at the inn, when I saw my father cornered helplessly, tormented, shamed and ridiculed, I did not come to his assistance and snatch him from his tormentor, the hunchback. Perhaps if I had told the truth in front of my father and all witnesses, out loud and unashamed, cried it to his very soul, if I had said that he was not a glory-covered general, but a military surgeon discharged for financial irregularities who now made himself the butt of scorn and mockery, I could have made him remember, could have saved him. I said nothing. I was afraid to speak. I had been struck mute by the hatred surrounding me, the barber's, Milada's, my father's hatred. Perhaps too, O God, something besides fear made me silent. Perhaps it was my lot, my fate to be the hunchbacked barber's confederate and the instrument of destruction.

My father avoided the stranger after that. In the morning, so as not to run into him, he slunk around outside the barbershop until he saw the stranger leave. His fear of meeting the stranger increased by the day. The barber not only noticed the agitation my father was in, he knew how to increase it. Usually he would tell my father that the "officer" — as the barber called the stranger — had asked about him.

"Asked about me?" My father looked dismayed. "Asked about me? Haschek, what does he want from me? Is there something he wants from me, Haschek?"

"I don't know a thing," the barber replied, "I don't know anything about it, Herr General. He only asked something like: 'What's that old Herr General up to?' But that was all he said."

"Was that all, dear Haschek, was that all?"

One day Haschek greeted the General beaming with joy. At last, he said, the officer had honored him with his full confidence. He had told him everything, but first he had bound him with a solemn oath of silence he would not break. Never would he divulge to a soul what the officer had told him about the purpose of his stay in our town.

"Not even me, Haschek?" my father asked.

"Herr General, I respectfully beg your pardon. Not even Herr General. Especially as it's a matter that doesn't concern Herr General, though it's interesting, very interesting."

"Doesn't concern me, my dear Haschek? Not me? Very well then, my dear Haschek!"

My father smiled. Surely he wished to probe no further. He was content. What business was the stranger of his, if he left him in peace? Now he could breathe easy again. But evidently the barber had expected to arouse my father's curiosity all the better with veiled insinuations. Finding himself disappointed, he was silent for a while, then began afresh. Having lathered my father's chin, he bent close to his ear:

"It's about a dismissed officer or something of the sort," he said.

My father's cheerful expression vanished. He seemed paralyzed by fear.

"Dismissed?"

"Yes, dismissed for irregularities. Apparently he lives around here somewhere. But I'm not allowed to say anything, Herr General."

"What is it, Haschek?"

"I'm not allowed to tell, Herr General. I promised him solemnly, Herr General."

"Tell me!"

"I respectfully report, Herr General, I'm not allowed to tell. Not even if Herr General were to command me, expressly command me . . ."

"I command you, Haschek," my father said faintly.

"O God, why did I mention it in the first place!" The hunchback made a helpless face. "Now I've got no choice but . . . But I must respectfully beg Herr General to keep the matter to himself. An official secret, Herr General. — Well, apparently there's a dismissed officer here, dismissed for accounting irregularities, and the officer has come to observe him and gather material . . ."

"Gather material?"

"Gather material against him."

My father sat frozen in the barber's chair, arms dangling. He looked at the hunchback with childish, fearful, imploring eyes.

"Dear Haschek," he said faintly, "dear Haschek."

Never did I feel more pain and more pity for my father than at that moment.

At the time I did not know the stranger's business in our town, but I knew it a few days later, when a certain incident led me to follow the stranger and observe him. This brings me to the point in my account at which I find it hard to continue. I feel that what I am about to relate, not the deed I was convicted for, reveals the very basest depths of my soul. Yet I can do nothing but report the facts without a word in extenuation and add how deep the shame of it is in my heart.

Ever since early childhood, and especially after returning from military school, I derived pleasure from tormenting animals. My usual victims were cats. More seldom dogs, and then only very young ones, still toothless. Barking dogs frightened me; otherwise I was indifferent to them. But I liked little puppies — still soft and toothless, fat and round as little moles, especially when still blind — almost as much as cats. Among cats I made no distinctions.

I believe in those years few cats in our town died a natural death. Most of them I must have tortured to death. I had different systems. The simplest was drowning. For this I had a special place by a pond not far from town. I proceeded as follows: I pulled from the pond a plank to which was tied the rotting corpse of a cat I had killed earlier, and tied my still-living cat on top of the dead one. Then I immersed the plank in such a way that the cat's lower body entered the water first. Then, very gradually — it often took an hour or more for the cat to drown — I lowered it into the water. Another system consisted of nailing the tails of two living cats to a plank, fixing this plank to a long nail jutting out from a wall and letting the cats dangle freely. With nothing to cling to, they clutched at each other, began to swing, sinking their claws into each other deeper and deeper until at last they tore each other to pieces. In a third method I proceeded by clamping the victim into a vice-like instrument I had made and stretching it until it died of its torments.

I could go on with descriptions of this kind for pages, but I think this suffices. I pray that this will show not the cruelty which filled my heart, but how unhappy I was and how lonely. Only here in prison has my heart found the path from unhappiness and isolation to peace, clemency and reconciliation; but it was ready for this path even then, when the blows of harsh experience drove it to such bitterness.

My treatment of animals led to the encounter with the stranger of which so much will be said later on. This is how it happened:

When I stalked a cat, I would first observe it for a long time as a hunter does his prey. This time I was tracking a tomcat, a fat black- and brown-spotted animal whose facial features have engraved themselves in my mind with particular vividness because of the incident which he occasioned and because he was my last victim. Cats' faces are not alike, any more than people's are. Now, the face of this tomcat made a kindly impression, as fat people's faces sometimes do. Do not smile if I speak of animals as if they were people. For just like people their faces reveal pain, joy, anger, and fear, only very few people are able to read animals' faces. I have read hatred in my victims' features, submission to fate, sometimes I have seen a ray of hope in their eyes. In this tomcat's face was kindness, and when he lay before me on the ground with injured limbs there was no anger in his face, no hatred; it was twisted as if with anguished tears.

I had observed that this cat crossed the roof of the house next to the inn every evening. I know the exact path he took, more or less down the middle of the roof's slope, about a meter below the scuttles. I sneaked up to the attic of the house, laid a noose in the cat's path, weighed it down with a stone and dropped the other end of the rope to the street. Then I left the attic to lie in wait on the street, holding the end of the rope in my hand. For several days, I waited in vain. In the evening quiet I always heard the cat's footsteps on the roof, but he did not step into the snare. At last, on about the fourth day, I felt a faint tug on the rope; I pulled, overcame the resistance with a jerk, and a moment later a dark mass came flying in an arc from the roof to the cobblestones of the square. I hurried up. The cat whimpered faintly. The noose had settled around his shoulders. Bending down, I regarded my victim for a moment. Then I picked up the rope, swung it through the air a few times with its burden and dropped it to the ground again. I did not know that someone was watching me. Just as I stepped on my victim's tail and pulled the rope to tighten the noose, the stranger walked up to me.

The stranger looked at me steadily for a moment. Perhaps he expected me, caught red-handed, to leave off at once or run away. But I did not avoid his eyes and I did not interrupt what I was doing. At that the stranger raised his hand and struck me twice in the face. Then he turned, silent as he had come, and walked away. At the same time I heard loud laughter behind me. I saw the hunchback, who must have been heading to the inn just now and had witnessed this scene.

I did not know what to do but crush the cat's head with the heel of my boot.

From the very beginning I had felt an aversion toward the stranger, this slender, well-built, elegant and self-confident man. Yet if this incident increased my aversion, it by no means turned the feeling into anger, as if at heart I took it for granted that a person like the stranger had the right to punish a person like me. In the days that followed, however, I observed the stranger closely and used every free moment to follow him unobtrusively. Perhaps I merely wanted to learn more about him to satisfy my curiosity, perhaps I hoped to find something to use against him; perhaps, though, I was drawn by the sheer desire to be near the stronger man, to dog his steps in hatred and love, to run the risk of encountering him.

I soon found out the reason for his presence in town. I

followed him on walks in the forest where he met a woman I knew. Some evenings I saw the stranger admit this woman into the inn through the back entrance, which lay on a narrow, deserted alley. If I had named this woman in court, she would have had to testify that I had not come to the stranger with the intent to commit murder on the day on which the murder ultimately occurred, that it was not my father who had followed me, as the hunchback testified, but I who had followed my father. For this woman was with the stranger when my father and I went to him. I was the only one who knew it. But I did not give her name.

I do not know whether the stranger noticed that I was following him and feared I might betray him, or whether indeed pity and remorse at his treatment of me moved him to write the letter which made me stop spying and turned my aversion into shy devotion. Another consequence of this letter was that I never abused animals again.

It was the only letter I have ever received in my life. About a week after my encounter with the stranger the postman brought it one morning before the barber arrived in the shop. When the barber found out about it later, he demanded to see the letter. He and the pregnant Milada pressed me to tell them who had written me and to show them the letter. But I refused. Then they beat me, threw me to the ground and searched my pockets. But I had hidden the letter in a crack in the floor.

The letter was addressed to the little soldier in Haschek's barbershop and said:

Dear Little Soldier!

They seem to know you by no other name here. If this name should offend you, do not take it amiss; I write it with the best of intentions, as I have not learned your true name, nor do I wish to inquire after it.

Don't be surprised that I am writing you. I could speak to you, too; after all, I see you every day in the barbershop where you work. Yet — for one thing I find it easier to write what I want to say to you, for another I do not want your master, who seems to have little love for you or me, to learn anything about what passes between us. Do not show him this letter, even if he asks you for it! Perhaps, little soldier, you think that because I hit you I am a happy man. Because without knowing you, without having the slightest idea who you are, I simply went up like that and hit you. Surely, you think, only a happy person can hit someone so thoughtlessly. But, little soldier, I am not a happy man, just as — I feel I know it for certain — you too are unhappy. Forgive me for hitting you instead of speaking with you. I do not know what sorrow, what pain, what loneliness, what desolation is inside you, that you go and torment innocent animals to death. Yesterday in my room I tore up books and clothes in pain and grief. And all at once I felt as if I understood you. And I decided to write to you so that you may forgive me.

You horrified me when I saw you with the poor cat. I will not ask what became of it afterwards. And yet I believe that you are not a murderer, but a poor, unhappy, homeless child. Perhaps you never had a mother. I almost want to pray to God to teach you forgiveness of your misfortune and yourself.

I hear that you wanted to become a soldier and have not yet abandoned the thought. I hope that your wishes will be fulfilled, little soldier. Here something was crossed out. I could not decipher it. Then the text went on: *But if you do not succeed, learn to understand that the time of hope is richer than the time of fulfillment.*

You will not understand why I am writing you, especially as some of what I have written may be unclear and hard to grasp. But even I, sitting in my room and thinking about you, comparing you to myself, am unable to account for everything; in me, too, all is not as clear and certain as it may seem to you.

Greetings, little soldier.

Stop torturing animals!

I did not show the letter to Milada and the barber. It said: "Do not show him this letter, even if he asks you for it!" And I never would have shown it, even if they had threatened to kill me. The stranger had no idea what I suffered for his sake, for a long time to come. But I was happy to suffer for him.

I never exchanged a word with the stranger, never replied to the letter, either in person or in writing. I caught a little kitten, tied a bow around its neck, put it in a box, bedded it down on sawdust and put a little pot of milk next to it. All this I laid at the stranger's doorstep.

In the meantime my father's state had altered drastically, and this showed outwardly as well. He seemed to have been seized by a tremendous unrest, unable to sit or stand still. His gaze, normally verging on rigidity, wandered about restlessly, his gait, normally measured and dignified, was hurried, his speech was disjointed, his voice was lowered to a whisper, his whiskers and clothes were unkempt. Almost all day my father hung about near the barbershop, slipping inside to whisper with the barber whenever the shop was empty. When the stranger left the barbershop in the morning, my father entered, glancing about warily, and looked anxiously for the barber. Haschek waved him over into a corner and, too quietly for me to hear, confided something which seemed to frighten my father all over again.

I think the hunchback whispered his communications so quietly into my father's ear not only to heighten the sense of mystery, but also because, seeing his barely-anticipated success with my father, he feared that I might thwart his plans. I admit that the hunchback could hardly have foreseen all that was to come. His plan was to humiliate my father more and more deeply through fright and fear of revelations, come of it what may.

The magnitude of the agitation that had seized my father struck me one evening at the inn. Once again I sat at the table by the door, my father at the table diagonally across from me, as before. The barber sat a few seats away from him at the same table, his back to the window. My father did not join in the conversation at first. He sat there smiling in all directions as if in apology. This smile made his face look helpless and more foolish than ever.

The gentlemen at my father's table whispered among themselves and snickered. The barber had probably drawn their attention to what my father was going through. One said:

"You're so quiet, Herr General!"

My father gave no reply, only went on smiling as before.

"Let's have a drink together, gentlemen," the gentleman said. "Herr General doesn't seem to be in the mood. Not in the right mood today!"

They ordered several bottles of wine and poured my father a glass. He drank swiftly and greedily. They all toasted him. A bit later the barber rose and left the room. After perhaps a quarter of an hour he returned. His face was grave, and he looked at my father, whose rigid smile now fled. He had drunk a great deal already, and his hands trembled when he raised the glass to his mouth. He had stretched out his feet, and kept his hands in his pockets when he was not drinking. The wine had made him regain his self-confidence. Now that he saw the barber return with such a grave expression, his eyes, glancing around so freely just now, were anxious again.

"What is it, Haschek?" my father asked.

"Oh, the stranger . . ." the hunchback said dismissively, irritably.

"What is it?"

"Let's not talk about it! Let's drink! Herr General, to your health, sir, most respectfully!"

My father raised the glass to his lips mechanically. But his hands trembled so hard that he spilled all the wine on his vest. He started, made a clumsy gesture as if to stop the liquid already spilling down his clothes, and dropped the glass, which broke with a crash. The gentlemen laughed.

"Herr General!"

My father had risen to his feet, looking at the hunchback,

while one of the guests at the table wiped his clothes with a napkin.

"What is it?" my father asked again, "dear Haschek, what is it?"

Someone pushed my father back into his seat.

"Gentlemen," said the barber, "a distinguished old officer dwells in our midst, a man living out his well-deserved retirement among us. But today his heart seems beset by troubles. Gentlemen, let us do our best to cheer up the worthy Herr General. Let us drink to his health!"

"What is it, dear Haschek?"

The gentlemen toasted my father, who hastily drained several glasses. They were civil servants from the district authorities, from the court, the town notary and two important merchants. I doubt that these gentlemen would ordinarily have shared a table with the hunchback, much less allowed him to monopolize the conversation. But as he knew best how to handle my father, how best to parade him in his absurdity, they tolerated it and even followed his instructions, much as one would follow the orders of an animal trainer parading a tamed animal, believing this to be the surest way of obtaining the anticipated pleasure.

"Gentlemen," the hunchback continued, "believe me, it rends my heart to think how bravery, service, sacrifice and loyalty are rewarded! I've happened to learn of a case, without knowing the names of those involved, however. An aging officer is being followed, hounded with investigations. Why, I ask you, why? Because those who hounded the old gentleman during the time of his service shy away from nothing in their persecution, not even the modest, unassuming happiness of his peaceful retirement. Why? Because they hate the righteous man who, rather than submit, preferred to shed the uniform worn in honor! Herr General, I respectfully beg your pardon for saying so much without permission. I am almost done. I am compelled to say what I believe. Gentlemen! I believe that Herr General also knows the matter I have hinted at and that his noble heart feels compassion for the innocent victim of ambitious intrigues. That is why Herr General is silent. Or perhaps, gentlemen, he thinks: what befalls you today, comrade — how easily might the victim have been the comrade of his bravery, one who stood by him in the hour of death on Europe's battlefields! — what befalls you today, comrade, can befall me tomorrow! And who will stand by me when I am attacked? Gentlemen, pledge Herr General your loyalty! He can be sure of my devotion. But what use am I to him, a hairdresser? You hold respected positions. Rise, approach this worthy man, solemnly pledge that you believe him and will stand by his side. We owe it to him, all of us. Without him the enemy might have ravaged our homeland and slaughtered us as youths and boys."

The hunchback paused. And the gentlemen rose and one at a time, with solemn tread and grave expressions, they went up to my father and shook his hand. At first my father seemed to have no idea what was going on, and he rose from his seat in great confusion. All at once he began to cry.

When they had all shaken his hand, the hunchback resumed:

"And I, too, Herr General, even if I am only a barber and

was never, due to my body's infirmity, found worthy of wearing even as a foot soldier the uniform Herr General wore through the decades, I respectfully beg permission to be the last to clasp and shake Herr General's hand."

He went up to my father, looked at him gravely and steadily and shook his hand:

"The hand of a worthy man!"

My father wiped the tears from his cheeks:

"Yes, yes," he said. "All the same."

They sat down again and started drinking. My father's spirits had lifted, perhaps from his companions' declaration of trust, perhaps from the wine. The others were in high spirits, in anticipation of the entertainment which this evening, so promisingly begun, might have in store. The barber, seeking to illustrate the world's ingratitude with a prominent example, spoke of Benedek.*

"A man we've all heard of!" he said.

"We've heard'f," my father mumbled.

"From Benedek?" asked the hunchback. "Herr General has heard from . . . ? Benedek wrote Herr General?"

"He wrote, dear Haschek."

"I beg respectfully, a letter?"

"Wrote a letter! Eight days ago a letter."

"Gentlemen, did you hear: Benedek — eight days ago — wrote Herr General a letter. Must have been an old brother in arms, seeking consolation, a friend, perhaps . . ."

"Perhaps, yes, yes."

"Herr General, I respectfully report, Herr General told us nothing of this."

"Told nothing, my dear Haschek. But all the same. Old comrade! Many a night, dear Haschek, slept in one bed, drank from one bottle, gentlemen, shared the last drop."

"And now, two such men," cried the hunchback, wringing his hands, "they send them packing, instead of letting them serve on for all of us, why, they even have them shadowed!"

"Yes, gentlemen, worthy men and they have them shadowed!" said my father, his speech already slurred. "Worthy men! Battles, gentlemen, skirmishes, looked death in the eye! They shy away from nothing! How Benedek wept when he told me of the investigation into the finances. Three hundred guldens, gentlemen. All paid up, but they shy away from nothing, they'd like to break his saber in the very grave."

"Investigation? Against Benedek?" asked the hunchback. "I beg respectfully, Herr General, when did he tell you this?"

"Eight days ago, gentlemen! Eight days ago. I can't believe my ears. What do you want? What do you want from a worthy man unaccustomed to keeping books, whose breast should be covered from top to bottom with the highest decorations," my father had risen to his feet, "yes, it should be covered from top to bottom with the highest decorations, this breast!"

At that moment the stranger entered and made straight for the table where he ate his supper every day. But my father turned and followed him. His feet dragged on the ground and he swayed. But he held himself erect.

"Yes indeed," he cried, looking at the stranger, "what do you want! This breast should be decorated with medals, sir, yes indeed, the breast of an old officer, yes indeed, all the same

. . . the breast of a worthy officer. Why are you persecuting him, sir, why are you persecuting him! How many campaigns, before you even saw the light of the world . . . yes, and you, what are you sneaking after him for? Believe him, he's innocent, he wants nothing, nothing, only peace, sir, peace, leave him in peace, let him be, I implore you, let him be!"

My father stood right in front of the stranger's table. Now his voice seemed choked with tears.

"All the same, a worthy officer! . . . Witnesses? Here they sit! They will defend me. Come, my friends, the time has come, come closer, defend him now, your friend. For that he is, your friend, and a worthy officer, all the same."

The stranger gazed in astonishment at my father, whom he must have taken for a madman. When my father leaned closer and closer to him without stopping, he rose, no doubt to put an end to the awkward scene, and quickly walked past my table into the kitchen. My father, his arms outstretched as if to embrace the stranger, stood motionless, staring after him in alarm and astonishment. For a moment my father's face twisted once again in that helpless forgiveness-seeking smile, then he collapsed sobbing upon the chair where the stranger had been sitting a moment before.

Then the hunchback rose and went up to my father. —

I come now to the description of the deed and the events immediately preceding it. Everything happened quickly, in the space of a few hours. I can do no more than describe the actual events as they happened. For it all happened so quickly. In these hours, joy, pain, passion, disgust, calm and hatred filled my heart in such succession that it is impossible for me to discover and explain their sequence. I feel that in this brief span of time all my life's forces were astir, good as well as evil. And I hope that those who understand me from this account will grasp it all, both what I say and what I cannot say because it is hidden from me as if by darkness. And understand why I shall attempt to describe the course of events as coolly as possible.

It was several days after that last scene at the inn; I was rolling down the shutters of our shop in the evening to go home. Milada and the barber had already left several hours before.

Our shop lay on the upper end of the market square. I walked slowly down the slightly sloping square. It was the last time. A few hours later I was under arrest.

When I had come about halfway, I saw my father hurrying across the square. I had no doubt that he was heading for the inn. Yet I stood where I was, gazing after him. And indeed he strode quickly toward the inn. At the door he stopped and looked all around. He seemed to hesitate, then darted into the house as if in sudden resolve.

I started on my way again, then stopped in alarm. Suddenly, perhaps because I was struck by my father's strange behavior, a thought came to me, immediately lodging in my mind and refusing to let me go. In fact, I thought, he didn't actually go into the taproom, he went upstairs! And already I had turned and was running toward the house into which my father had vanished.

I wanted to prevent my father from humiliating himself in front of the stranger again. I felt completely devoted to the stranger now, and after he had seen me as a sadistic cat-murderer, I did not want him now to behold my father in his profound debasement. I did not want my father to shame me anew in front of the stranger.

My hunch had not deceived me. As soon as I entered the broad carriage-entrance of the inn, I heard my father's loud voice above. I ran up the stairs and went through the door without knocking.

The stranger, dressed in elegant pajamas, stood facing my father in apparent bafflement. I saw at once that my father had been drinking. A little kitten playing in the corner caught my eye, and I was glad to see it. But at the same time I glimpsed a woman's clothing on an armchair, and saw that someone was hiding in the bed. I knew who it was.

The stranger looked at me happily, as if I had come to rescue him. I sullenly avoided his eyes. I knew what he was afraid of: that the woman in his bed might be discovered. At that moment I felt repugnance toward him, risen just now from this woman's side.

My father also seemed glad to see me.

"You see!" he cried out tearfully. "My son, my poor child. If you have no pity upon the father, spare his poor, unfortunate, innocent son!"

I went up to my father.

"Be silent, sir!" I said angrily.

"But what do you want?" asked the stranger. "What do you want from me?"

"Nothing but pity, mercy! Stop what you are doing, I

beseech you, and spare me! Yes, I am guilty! But you, you are young . . . you don't know! Don't sit in judgment! Over a worthy, battle-tried . . . Believe a battle-tried officer! A gray head, a poor child, sir, have mercy, promise me . . . !"

"But my dear sir, it is not for me to pardon . . . !"

At that my father fell to his knees before the stranger. He stretched his hands out toward him. The stranger fell back a step.

"Mercy, spare me, a gray head, sir, a gray head. Have pity, sir, on the child, sir, on the child!"

Sobbing, he slid toward the stranger on his knees and reached out his hand for the stranger's hand. But the stranger pulled it away. Then my father bowed his head as if to kiss the stranger's shoes.

Trembling, I grabbed my father by the arm.

"Stand up, sir, and come with me!" I said.

My father looked at me sullenly and tried to break loose from my hand. I shook him as if to rouse him.

"Stand up, Father!" I was angry and ashamed.

"No, no," my father cried, "first pardon me. I'm guilty, but pardon me. I won't get up until you do. Mercy . . . my gray hair!"

Again my father bent down sobbing to the stranger's feet, shod in red slippers.

I dragged my father into an upright position and looked him in the face. I saw tears trickle from his eyes and into his beard.

"Come!" I shouted, and when my father went on crying, I hit him in the face.

At that my father stood up. Suddenly his face was grave. He seized me.

"Come!" he said, and we went.

When we stepped outside, my father stopped, still holding me.

"You struck your father," he said. "It will be your death. Come!"

We crossed the square to our house, and I was not afraid. There was no doubt in my mind that my father would kill me now, and yet I was not afraid. I was filled with joy. I thought that now my father would take from the cabinet the old service pistol I had often cleaned, load it and turn it upon me. I rejoiced and thought of Roman commanders who had killed their sons.

My mood changed as I climbed the dark stairs to our apartment, my father still dragging me by the sleeve. I heard voices and recognized Milada and the barber. They sat in our living room. Bottles and glasses stood on the table. Milada no longer seemed sober. Probably my father had been drinking with them before he went to the stranger.

As soon as we entered the room my father said:

"He struck his father. He must die!"

"Struck his father? You!" The hunchback shoved me in the chest. "Did you hear, you're going to die!"

I don't believe the barber would have let it come to that.

Drunken Milada pressed up against me. I pushed her away. She was pregnant, and that increased my loathing of her.

My father had taken his pistol from the cabinet. His

hands trembled so violently that he was unable to load it. The hunchback had retreated to the back of the room. He was afraid of firearms. So I loaded the pistol and laid it on the table. Now Haschek came back out of his corner.

"Let's drink!" he said.

"And him?" My father pointed to me.

"He must die. But first let's drink!"

"Let him watch," cried Milada, "watch us drinking. Let's tie him to the door! Let's tie him!"

She crowded me against the open door of the bedroom. The hunchback found a rope. They wrapped the rope around my feet, pulled it tight and tied it around the door-hinge. At first I swayed, unable to stand. But then I got used to it, however badly my feet hurt, and held myself upright.

They yelled and drank. My father had fallen silent, but he drank a great deal as well. He sat on the old sofa until he fell over. Milada swore at me constantly. One time she got up and spat in my face. When I tried to wipe away the spit, she threw a wine glass at me, making my forehead bleed. I covered my face with my hands. Then she cried that I shouldn't cover my face and tried to pull my hands away. Her gravid body touched mine and made me shudder. She called over the hunchback to help her. I did not resist the hunchback. But her I pushed away.

At that she cried out, ordered the barber to hold me and tore jacket and shirt from my body. She punched my naked chest until my breath failed me. Then she opened my pants so I stood there naked. I writhed in the barber's hands. Milada felt me.

"A man," she cried, "look, a man already!"

She laughed.

"He's excited! Let's cool him off."

She poured wine over my member and laughed.

She laughed harder and harder, spasmodic, ghastly laughter. The hunchback let me go. I pulled up my pants.

But Milada began to twist and scream. Then she tore off her skirts and dropped to the ground with a scream.

It happened that she went into labor.

The hunchback quickly cut my hobble.

"Keep an eye on things!" he said. "I'll run and get a doctor."

Unable to walk at first, I fell to the floor. Then I rose. Milada lay on the floor, writhing, legs splayed. She had raised her shift and held the hem clenched in her teeth, exposing her distended body. I saw blood between her feet. She tossed in agony. I took the pistol from the table. My eyes fell upon my father.

My father lay on the black sofa with his eyes closed. His head hung to the side. A thin green ribbon of phlegm and spittle trickled from his open mouth. For a moment I felt that I must kill my father at once. I would have shortened that poor man's life by just three days.

Milada, whose feet I heard drumming the floor, cried out. Then it was quiet.

I went up to Milada.

A filthy bloody gob lay between her feet in a puddle of blood and foul-smelling liquid. I looked at the baby. It whimpered so thinly that one could scarcely hear it. It made me think of very young kittens. I was still holding the pistol.

I heard steps on the stairs and thought it was the hunchback returning. A knock came at the door. I did not answer.

Then the door opened and the stranger entered the room.

I looked at him in alarm. He was wearing patent leather shoes, pressed pants, a snug winter coat and a green felt hat. I stood there between a father drunk out of his senses and a newborn child that lay in blood and filth between the splayed legs of the unconscious mother, not yet severed from her. My torso was bare and beaten bloody. The stranger could see my flat chest and my crooked back. I thought of his red slippers. I raised the pistol and shot.

The stranger collapsed without a cry. I took some of the cotton-wool my father stuffed into his ears every day, dipped it in water, and carefully washed Milada's child.

The hunchback entered with the doctor. They stumbled across the stranger immediately.

"Who did that?" asked the doctor.

"There." The hunchback pointed at me, smiling.

"Call the police!"

"Don't be afraid!"

They bent over Milada.

"She must be put to bed," said the doctor. "I'll fetch my things and tell the police at once." His eye fell upon my father. "What's this?"

"Stinking drunk" said the barber.

"And . . . the pistol there?"

"You can leave it where it is. Nothing will happen. I'll stay here."

When the doctor had gone, the hunchback took a bill from his pocket.

"Run away," he said.

But I did not run away. I sat down by the window and waited.

colbert's journey

COLBERT'S JOURNEY

Colbert began his journey in 1910. He died in 1911 from its attendant excitations. Modlizki had disappointed him too bitterly. Colbert's grave can be found in the town cemetery. It consists of a white marble cross and bears the simple inscription:

Here lies Josef Colbert
born March 14, 1859, here,
died May 7, 1911, in the very same place

According to this, he lived to the age of fifty-two.

His journey finds no mention in the inscription.

What made Colbert's disappointment all the more bitter was that Modlizki had grown up in his household since early childhood. Modlizki was of lowly birth — his father was a drunkard and had departed this life in ignominious fashion. He was caught at a burglary, fell from a ladder, and died at once without receiving absolution for his final sin. Modlizki did not bear him in fond memory and bashfully avoided discussing his origins.

Colbert, by contrast, boasted French blood. His great-grandfather, he said, had emigrated from Nancy. Colbert claimed to possess a document to that effect. He smiled patronizingly at his fellow citizens' manners and mores and let his superiority show outwardly. He wore his goatee in the French style and twirled up his moustache at the ends. He washed his head with fragrant colognes that were said to make his bald pate gleam tender and rosy and feel as soft as a fine velvet cloth. And Colbert interlarded his speech with French words, even if he possessed no large assortment of them. He deemed this proper for a man of the world, and held that it gave one's eloquence a cosmopolitan touch. He discussed the point at length with Modlizki, who listened attentively and from time to time expressed his agreement with a respectful nod, not daring, out of a perhaps misguided notion of modesty, to ask his master and benefactor for a fuller explanation of this view.

Modlizki performed all duties in the little house on the outskirts of town where Colbert lived with his wife and daughter. He was the porter, he tended the little front garden, followed Frau Colbert to the market and carried the heavy bag, washed clothes and cleaned shoes, and even helped the women in the kitchen, for he was the household's only servant. He had been taken in as a child by the then-childless couple, and his status in the household had always been a peculiar one. After carrying in the serving dishes from the kitchen, he ate at the family table with the others. But he sat quietly in prudent restraint, replying only when asked a question. As soon as the meal was over Modlizki rose and left the room, first bowing silently in the direction of the table. Every day Colbert rejoiced anew in his servant's well-bred modesty and returned his salute with a smile. Modlizki washed the dishes in the kitchen.

Until the age of forty Colbert had run the business his father left him, a sizable grocery. At forty he had bought a house in the newly-built cottage tract and retired from mercantile life. He had conducted and wrapped up his affairs felicitously, and his daughter would come into a respectable inheritance one day. Colbert's daughter had been christened Amélie. Much to Colbert's displeasure, this did not prevent her mother from simply calling the child Maltscha, adapting the rather unusual name to common parlance.

"Mon dieu," Colbert would say, "what are you doing to my only child's name, Mélanie?"

But Milena Colbert, his wife, paid no heed to his remonstrances. Sometimes she gave a scornful shrug instead of answering, and sometimes she retorted tartly: "Leave me in peace with your notions. We're the laughingstocks of the town as it is."

At that Colbert buttoned up his jacket all the way to the top and left the room. He went down the stairs and glanced into Modlizki's room. When Modlizki was not there, he found him in the garden. He complained to him about his wife's lack of understanding. Modlizki regarded his master calmly, and when Colbert, seeking comfort, asked his opinion, he would say: "We must endure it, Herr Colbert."

This moved Colbert deeply — be it that he was already emotional in such moments, be it that Modlizki's "we" showed Colbert how greatly all that affected him affected his servant as well, and the sudden ebullition was provoked by the mounting sensation that he was not alone and had a companion in woe. Touched, Colbert shook Modlizki's hand.

It was at such a moment that Colbert chose Modlizki as his companion and revealed to him the plans for the journey.

They stood in Modlizki's room, a chamber with one window containing nothing but Modlizki's bed, a wardrobe, and the picture of a saint. For a moment Colbert looked at Modlizki without a word. He was breathing heavily.

"Come," he said then, resolute.

He led him to the attic, stopping in front of a locked door. He took the key from his pocket and opened it.

They entered a small room dimly lit by a skylight. Colbert turned to Modlizki.

"Here," he said.

He clutched Modlizki by his jacket-button.

"Now I will confide in you, mon cher! C'est la secret de ma vie! It is the secret of my life!"

His voice was earnest and solemn.

Modlizki had inclined his head with the close-cropped black hair.

"I know you are devoted to me," said Colbert. "I took you in from the cloister orphanage when you were six years old and raised you as my own child. Mon enfant, you will not betray me!" He fought back tears.

"Do you mean to forget my lowly birth?" Modlizki said quietly.

"Quelle naïveté, mon ami! Who is speaking of that?" Colbert paced up and down the room. When he came near the skylight, where the roof was lower, he had to bow his head. "Who is speaking of your birth? You must not breathe a word of what I tell you, Modlizki, do you understand me, as-tu compris?"

Modlizki gave a measured nod. His eyes regarded Colbert, big and solemn. This look of Modlizki's was the only thing Colbert disliked about his servant, though Modlizki's eyes were the finest feature of his face. His nose was long, his complexion brownish-yellow. But Modlizki's eyes were set beneath long-drawn black brows, they were long-lashed and themselves big and black. Colbert could not account for his abhorrence of Modlizki's gaze. It seemed to remind him of something unpleasant. These eyes rested steadily on Colbert. When Modlizki stood before him like this, dressed in black, his head slightly bowed, the very picture of restrained modesty, this gaze was alien to Colbert and incommensurate.

"It's improper," thought Colbert, turning away. For a moment he stared silently through the tiny aperture of the skylight. Then he turned back to Modlizki.

"Bon," he said. "I trust you, Modlizki." He paused for a moment. Then he said slowly, emphasizing every word: "I have decided to take a journey."

He fell back a few steps and looked at Modlizki. But Modlizki's demeanor remained unchanged. Could it be that Modlizki hadn't understood?

"I am going to take a journey, Modlizki! Here!" he said, pointing to a pile of books stacked up in the corner.

Modlizki came closer.

"Paris!" Colbert swallowed the final "s."

They were French textbooks, phrasebooks for travelers,

Baedeckers, guides to Paris and illustrated catalogues of art collections and museums.

"This is all a secret, Modlizki! It's been long in preparation. Here," he leafed excitedly through the books, "I work here every day. It will be a long journey. It will be a journey on the order of months, mon ami. Three months, easily four, c'est possible."

Again he paced up and down.

"You shall accompany me, Modlizki." He gave him a penetrating look.

"I?"

Colbert nodded earnestly.

"When will we depart?" asked Modlizki.

"Oh, as soon as everything's ready," said Colbert briskly, "oh, many preparations remain to be made. After all, one must be prepared for everything, Modlizki. We will work together every day now. But *attention*, that Mélanie doesn't notice! She would sabotage it. Paris, Modlizki, Paris, don't you understand! The Louvre, have you never heard of the Louvre? We will see everything, Modlizki, oh, these paintings, here, here, just glance through this book, these treasures, la France, la France! How can you fail to grasp it! C'est à s'arracher les cheveaux! Oh, this is the price you pay for your birth, I make you no reproaches, you are not to blame, Modlizki, you will understand when you see it, Modlizki, then you will be as moved as I am, and your heart will beat as fast as mine."

He clutched Modlizki by the shoulder.

Modlizki stood bent over by the skylight, leafing through the book Colbert had thrust into his hands. His eyes skimmed the reproductions of paintings, statues and buildings.

"Perhaps you are right, Herr Colbert, to remind me of my father and my mother," said Modlizki. "Perhaps this really is only for those of good family and not for people of such lowly birth. I had better stay at home, Herr Colbert. A man's presence may be required for the protection of the household. Your enjoyment will be greater alone."

"Everything's been thought of," said Colbert. "I will ask my wife's cousin to stay. Everything's been thought of. After long reflection I have reached the decision to take you with me. A journey involves much that is unforeseen. It is well to have a companion, just in case. I am not thinking of the worst, no, not at all. But aren't there always occasions when one wishes to confer with another, trustworthy person? You see, Modlizki! One is often confronted with unexpected situations. Enfin, two heads are better than one, that too is important when you are all on your own. But now it is time to make the final arrangements. What to pack — a difficult task requiring ample reflection, mon dieu, who would have thought it! Then the language: to be prepared for all eventualities. Here are compilations containing all the necessary phrases, the choice of trains, the hotels, the schedule, O mon enfant, there are a thousand possibilities, and one must always choose the best."

Frau Colbert's voice was heard calling for Modlizki.

"Yes, yes, depêche-toi, go, mon fils," said Colbert, "and breathe not a word!"

Modlizki closed the door behind him. Colbert remained behind in the little room. He sat down exhausted on the stack of books and wiped the sweat from his brow with a perfumed handkerchief.

We know nothing of Modlizki's thought processes. Outwardly Modlizki's behavior did not change. Colbert, though, was a changed man from the day he revealed his plan to Modlizki. He sat smiling at the dinner table and treated Mélanie with a courtesy still more exquisite than usual. At meals he often nodded amiably at Modlizki. Modlizki gave a silent look in return without changing the expression on his face.

Once, soon after the conference in the attic, Colbert said at the table: "Happy was the day we took him in, was it not, ma chérie?"

Milena Colbert did not reply. She gazed severely at the platter of meat in front of her and merely screwed up her mouth; she disliked Modlizki and despised Colbert's prattle. She was given to speaking to Maltscha of her father disdainfully, as if she had every right to hold the daughter responsible for the father's character.

"He's getting more childish by the day," she said. "Soon we'll be putting him in a baby carriage and sticking a pacifier in his mouth."

Twice a day she had a special opportunity to fume at her husband. That was after each meal. Once he had officially ended the meal Colbert insisted upon kissing the hand of his unwilling and indignant wife with a graceful bow. He applied all his adroitness to seizing a favorable moment. Milena's spiteful words did not deter him.

"I owe it to myself," he said to Modlizki.

Milena took Colbert's childish behavior as a personal insult.

What followed on Modlizki's part is inexplicable. It will be seen how Colbert's death was caused by the actions of this person who had been raised like a child of the household. There is no explanation of Modlizki's sudden outburst of enmity and hatred, for he spoke plainly of it to no one. Even Amélie, who, on closer terms with Modlizki than anyone else, should have been the first to know, failed to understand Modlizki's obscure hints. She was barely fifteen years old at the time. Yet she already had well-developed breasts and was as tall as her mother.

When Colbert was long dead and Modlizki long vanished, Amélie often discussed the events of those months with her disconsolate mother. She described the changes she had noticed in Modlizki. That was not enough to explain why Modlizki had suddenly erupted in malice and baseness. For her part, Frau Colbert, who always called her daughter Amélie now, did not doubt that Modlizki had always harbored this hatred in his heart, carefully concealed. He had never smiled. And when Amélie sat down at the piano after dinner at her parents' behest, Modlizki left the room. Frau Colbert had seen his look of malice. There was no other reason for it all but the innate hatred of the low-born toward the noble and pure, as exemplified in the life of a good middle-class family.

"He was noble, Amélie," said Frau Colbert, lifting a handkerchief to her eyes. "How gladly we forgave him his childish whims. They were simply the expression of his amiable nature."

Amélie had reason to reproach herself. Her only excuse was her youth. Had she told everything in time, Modlizki would have been exposed before it was too late. For Amélie had been visiting Modlizki in his room since the age of fourteen. She used the time after dinner, when her parents were asleep. Amélie had never spoken of these visits. She was deeply ashamed of them. Even in her later years the thought of them tormented her.

At first Modlizki merely showed Amélie pictures in his room. They were photographs he kept locked in a casket. This casket in turn lay at the bottom of a black wooden trunk under the bed. The pictures showed naked men and women, sometimes depicted separately, sometimes in combination with one another. Later Modlizki also unclothed himself before Amélie and instructed her in the nature and purpose of the human organs. He mentioned that he intended to attempt with Amélie what the pictures showed in such variety, but he left the time unclear. What he was waiting for is not known. Amélie feared that moment greatly. Nonetheless, she put up no resistance to Modlizki's pronouncements. That was what she was most ashamed of later.

All this is mystifying. Modlizki had enjoyed a religious upbringing in the cloister before Herr Colbert took him in. He wore an amulet around his neck and frequently went to confession. No doubt only Modlizki's birth explains this character trait of his.

About the time Colbert initiated Modlizki into the plan of his journey, Modlizki suddenly began to call Amélie Maltscha in her parents' absence. Amélie was struck by the coincidence, though a connection will be difficult or impossible to discern. But Amélie ascribed great significance to this fact later on, even if she could not say what this significance was.

With Amélie, Modlizki made no secret of Herr Colbert's announcement. Despite having sworn secrecy, he told her that very same day. Amélie recalled that he called her Maltscha then for the first time. He was ill-tempered that day and said little.

Every day at ten in the morning Modlizki had to repair to the attic room. Herr Colbert awaited him there in a state of excitement. These days his mood was extremely volatile. Now he was quiet, as if surrendering himself to great and grave thoughts, now he was cheerful, even exuberant, joking with Amélie and Modlizki.

On these mornings the preparations for the journey were made. Colbert could not get his fill of rhapsodizing to Modlizki about Paris and France. It pained him to see how unaffected Modlizki was by the magnitude of the moment. Modlizki remained grave and impassive and watched Herr Colbert silently as he paced back and forth in the low room.

Colbert talked everything over with his servant. He seemed to be spending sleepless nights mulling over the journey, and always had something new to discuss with Modlizki in the morning. All the while new books with tips for travelers were arriving, catalogues, guides, even a book on first aid in case of accidents and a small first-aid kit. Herr Colbert himself secretly collected these parcels at the post office.

As a rule he started talking as soon as Modlizki came in, as if continuing a conversation already begun.

"It would be best," he said, "to book the large pieces of luggage through to Paris. Insured, naturellement. We will have reserved the room in the Hotel Mercure in advance. Then the duty can be paid in Paris. You won't take it into your head to pack dutiable items, Modlizki! Oh, quel horreur, if we were to be penalized! I beg you, don't think of it, Modlizki! C'est blamable! It would lose us a whole morning in Paris, c'est vrai. Mais, better than standing there at the border with lots of luggage. One also hears of thefts occurring during the inspections at the border. It's better this way, don't you think?"

Modlizki nodded.

"I believe we understand each other," said Colbert. "We will travel splendidly, mon camarade! But one more thing, my dear fellow, mon très cher, understand me rightly. C'est une chose délicate, mon ami. A delicate matter. You know that Paris is a big city, une ville mondiale, with all possible allurements and seductions. When traveling, a person is in a state of extreme excitement, think of the Louvre, Modlizki, of the street life, it could happen that he succumbs to this temptation. Don't sneer at my age. In such moments, c'est admirable, you feel the vigor of youth course through your veins. But there's a great danger that one could be abducted to the darker quarters of the city, and leave them robbed or not at all. You understand me, my son, you understand me, don't you, tu saisis?"

Modlizki inclined his head in affirmation.

"You have known me for many years now, Modlizki. You know that I am not the frivolous sort. I revere my wife, my family. Parole d'honneur, it's the last thing I would do. But, my dear fellow, an extraordinary occasion demands extraordinary measures. C'est une affaire extraordinaire. One must take everything into account when traveling. I believe I have thought of everything. One must be forearmed."

He paced up and down and wiped his forehead with the handkerchief. It was very warm in the attic.

"Open the window, Modlizki," said Colbert.

"Well, well," he went on, "it must be taken care of beforehand. One must discharge one's tension beforehand, do you understand me, Modlizki, do you understand me, mon dieu, please try to see what I am saying!"

"I still don't understand you, Herr Colbert," said Modlizki.

Colbert stepped up to Modlizki. He grasped him by the shoulder and looked at him.

"Modlizki," he said, "as I said, c'st une chose délicate, mais nécessaire. A girl from our town lives in Prague, where she is said to have fallen into loose ways. You know who it is. You shall ascertain her address and summon her to the train, all as if for yourself, of course. I have precautions to take. You shall write to her, Modlizki, and arrange the price at once. Don't sneer!"

Modlizki did not sneer; he made his modest gesture of understanding and agreement.

"Do you know what I'd like," Modlizki said to Maltscha that afternoon. "I'd like to call your darling mother 'Sow!' at the dinner table."

Amélie recoiled.

"Oh God, oh God, Modlizki! What has she ever done to you? Why, Modlizki?"

"The fuss you people make gets on my nerves," said

Modlizki. "There he goes raving on about his Louvre, his travels. What concern is it of mine? I'm his servant, and I do what he asks of me."

"Why does that get on your nerves, Modlizki?"

"Because he doesn't understand that it's none of my concern. Because he demands that I join in the fuss. What concern is it of mine?"

"I don't understand all that, Modlizki," said Amélie.

Modlizki gave no reply. Possibly he did not understand it himself.

Colbert prepared every last detail of the journey in Modlizki's presence. These preparations lasted for weeks. Excerpts were taken from the guides, the necessary phrases were alphabetized and indexed; finally a new trunk of large dimensions was smuggled up to the attic one evening and several valises and suitcases were gotten ready. Then the quantity of clothing, the number and type of garments was discussed and decided upon. They were put in the suitcases. And at last the day of departure was set. It was to be a Wednesday. For a number of reasons this day struck Colbert as most propitious for the start of a journey. Saturday, Sunday and Monday were out of the question, for experience showed that on these days more people traveled than usual. Thursday was the town's market-day and thus it, too, was an unfavorable day for traveling. One could perfectly well avoid beginning a journey on Friday without being superstitious, because one can hold a prejudice without believing in it. This left the choice between Tuesday and Wednesday, and it fell on Wednesday for a compelling reason. On Wednesday Frau Colbert was very busy all day. Every Wednesday a woman came early in the morning to clean the house and wash the floors. Herr Colbert had reason to hope that on a Wednesday his wife would have no time to concern herself much with him and put a stop to the journey. And if he informed her of his departure with Modlizki at lunch on Wednesday, it could be assumed that she would have less time and inclination to pursue the matter than on ordinary days. Perhaps her husband's departure would not even sink in until Thursday.

Several days before that Wednesday Herr Colbert said to Modlizki: "We shall travel second class, Modlizki! And for a number of reasons. Firstly, it is less taxing and we will arrive in better spirits, and secondly, it is agreeable to travel in the company of those who belong to the educated classes, perhaps meeting persons of learning and refinement, the acquaintance with whom is both pleasant and profitable. One often hears of such things happening on journeys. At first I thought of having you travel third class, but I do not wish to be parted from you, Modlizki."

"It seems to me," replied Modlizki, "that your initial thought was more proper, Herr Colbert. I do not belong in the second class, where men and women of the better stations travel. Who am I without you, Herr Colbert, if you think about it! Ought I to be accustomed to such things when I am alone one day?"

"Alone?" asked Colbert.

"Now, Herr Colbert, I know you will not neglect me in your will. But you cannot rob Fräulein Amélie. You are a rich man; you travel for pleasure. You will travel second class. But I am not traveling to see the things you wish to see. I am traveling as your servant and companion."

"Oh, mon cher, what kind of talk is that, Modlizki? You will travel as I do, Modlizki. You will see what I see, all the wonders of Paris, your heart will beat faster as mine does, je suis ton père, Modlizki, am I not like a father to you?"

Modlizki bowed.

"Yet it seems to me, Herr Colbert," he said with deliberation, "that a man of my station does not travel. Travel is a pleasure for the rich man. A man of my station travels from necessity, or like me, in service. He should remain where he was born, for that is where he belongs, it seems to me."

"You must see everything as I do, Modlizki."

"I do not know how it befits me to see everything, Herr Colbert. I am of lowly birth. You know that my father . . ."

"Why are you bringing that up? Comme c'est horrible, Modlizki!"

"Perhaps it needs to be brought up," Modlizki persisted. "My mother was blind. You know how she was blinded. You know that my father hit her on the head so hard she lost her sight. She is in a home for the blind. I have no relations with her. My father did not do it without cause. He found her with Herr Kudernak, who claimed to have paid her handsomely for it. Herr Kudernak was much laughed at, for my mother was neither beautiful nor clean. Herr Kudernak lives here, enjoying his pension. He would make a good companion."

"Modlizki," said Colbert, "Modlizki!"

"I only meant to say," and Modlizki bowed, "that it would

better befit me to travel third class. But if you wish otherwise, Herr Colbert, I will do my best to overcome the restraint that is proper to me."

"All that will change," said Colbert, suddenly cheerful again. "Nous verrons! As soon as you have seen these wonders! Raphael's Madonnas, the Venus de Milo, the Palace of Versailles and that splendid city. Mon ami, how such a journey enriches one!"

The day Colbert and Modlizki were to depart drew near. Colbert hardly ever left the attic now. He sat by the suitcases Modlizki had packed. He was in a state of perpetual emotion and hugged and kissed Modlizki several times. Modlizki submitted with modest resistance. Colbert searched all the bags for his notes and lists, which he continually thought he had forgotten. Modlizki sewed the money into a little bag that Herr Colbert planned to wear around his neck. Colbert spoke incessantly of Paris. Sometimes it struck Modlizki as rather incoherent. On the last evening before their departure Colbert wept long and uncontrollably. Modlizki did not try to comfort him.

No attempt will be made to explain the things that will now be related. They happened unexpectedly, and probably they cannot be explained or justified at all. It will simply be told how one thing happened after another at lunch on this critical Wednesday.

Herr Colbert appeared punctually. Modlizki was still setting the table. Herr Colbert took his seat and gave Modlizki a faint nod. Modlizki saw that his master's face was without color, as if all the blood had fled it. Frau Colbert did not notice, and it seemed to escape Amèlie as well. The spoon trembled so hard in Herr Colbert's hand that he put it down without tasting the soup.

From time to time Herr Colbert turned and looked at Modlizki. Modlizki gazed at him impassively.

After the soup Herr Colbert sat up straight. He turned to his wife. He spoke in a quiet voice. "Ecoutez, mon bijou, vous êtes ravissante aujourdhui," he said, "listen, my dear."

It looked as if he were about to put his hand on Milena's. But he stopped halfway.

"Listen, I have an announcement to make to you . . . I am leaving on a journey today . . ." He spoke louder, as if to screw up his courage with the sound of his voice. "To Paris, ma bonne."

Frau Colbert put down her spoon and looked at her husband in silence.

Herr Colbert shifted uneasily on his chair.

"To Paris," he said, "all the arrangements have been made, ma chère . . . Here . . . here . . ." he searched his pockets. "Here are the tickets. Modlizki is coming with me. Aren't you, Modlizki . . . Say something, Modlizki!"

Modlizki looked from one to the other. At last his gaze lingered on Herr Colbert, whose brow was bathed in sweat. Modlizki smiled.

"Permit me to remark that I fail to understand your excitement, Herr Colbert. Your Louvre can't be that important, Herr Colbert, certainly not to me."

Colbert stared at him wide-eyed. He did not seem to understand him.

"And while I'm at it, Herr Colbert, permit me to tell you one more thing. Namely, that I have decided not to come."

It can hardly be supposed that Modlizki had reached this decision before that very moment. He had never mentioned anything of the kind to Amélie.

Colbert slumped back in his chair.

"Modlizki," he said tonelessly, "Modlizki."

There was a profound silence.

Inexplicable things must have passed through Modlizki's mind at that moment. Amélie could not recall ever in her life having seen a face as horribly distorted and convulsed as Modlizki's then. A taut sinew twitched faintly in his right cheek. His eyes fixed on Herr Colbert maliciously.

The only possible conclusion is that Modlizki was considering at that moment how to wound Colbert most deeply. No one will be able to find a reason for it. For a moment his eyes lingered maliciously on Amélie. She lowered her eyes. Perhaps he thought of getting up and grabbing Amélie's breasts in front of her parents. Suddenly Modlizki's features relaxed, and he broke the profound silence by conducting himself out loud in a way which, in this household, was known at the very most in Herr and Frau Colbert's bedroom. Then Modlizki rose and left the room and the house without a parting word.

Amélie had turned red. A stern look from her mother bade her withdraw.

For a long time Colbert sat motionless, staring in front of him absently. Then he slowly shook his head.

"That is the wind of insurrection," he said tonelessly.

He fainted. Frau Colbert had to take him to bed with Amélie's help.

Colbert died soon after. It seems he was unable to recover from this disappointment. He had an overly sensitive nature.

This happened in the year 1911. But one could say that Colbert began his journey, on which through Modlizki's fault he was never to embark, the year before.

The inscription on his gravestone was already mentioned.

THE WINE-TRAVELER

I do not wish to dwell upon the impressions of my youth. Suffice it to say that I was born thirty-six years ago as the son of a traveling salesman. Early on I acquired the skills which would one day enable me to take over my father's business. Though he had struggled all his life to make ends meet, he had a great legacy to leave me: his knowledge of the clientele. He knew all potential customers in his district — and there were potential customers in the smallest towns — not only by name, he knew their relatives, family background and character traits. That is no easy matter in a trade as far-flung as the wine trade. One must call upon the innkeepers in the small towns, grocers and hoteliers in the cities. It's a colorful lot the wine-traveler meets on his job, more colorful than the clientele of, say, the traveler in cloth. Innkeepers are scoundrels, people say, and the truth of it is that the innkeeper has a more checkered métier than any other merchant.

If I felt called to write a novel plumbing the depths of the human heart, I would make my hero an innkeeper. The owner, say, of a small hotel. It would lie on a narrow side street, among music halls and little shops. The secrets of such a house, the people who pass in and out, lovers and black marketeers, the to and fro of grim or laughing figures, the leaven of the people and the cream of high society — and in their midst the innkeeper, outwardly the petty bourgeois, but his heart filled with the secrets of a clientele which tempts him to demand more of life than is his lot.

Ultimately there is no difference between a hotelier in the capital and an innkeeper in the provinces. The stage is smaller, the drama played out by fewer actors, but the passions are just as hot and consuming. I would venture that the innkeeper in the provinces has one thrill which gives him the advantage over the hotelier in the capital: the stranger from the capital who connects him to the wide world, whose luggage he scrutinizes with the same sensual curiosity as his clothes and his linens in the closet. It is hard to fool an innkeeper. If the con men's guild had a test for mastery, no doubt the task would be to coax a penny from an innkeeper.

I say this because the profession has played a special role in my life, as we shall see, and to convey how difficult the wine-traveler's business is, quite apart from the fact of dealing in wine. Wine is called merchandise, just as silk and paper are called merchandise, though paper and silk of a certain grade and color can be produced ad infinitum, and one piece of the same type and grade of paper will always look exactly the same as another. Knowing paper and silk is a matter of practice. A wine-traveler is born, not made. Knowing wine is a mysterious gift. It hinges not only on the refinement of the taste buds. That is an obvious requirement. I do not hesitate to call this gift a gift of the heart. It cannot be trained, learned or analyzed. Is it presumptuous of me to compare it with artistic inspiration, which, too, cannot be learned, but is simply there, a gift of the gods? It is not creative like the poet's gift. But isn't there also uncreative artistry, the art of enjoyment, of response, isn't it — the ability to be intoxicated by music, say, the ecstasy of the listener — like the gift of the creative artist, granted to few, and as stirring as the gift of the creator? And isn't something of the creative force inherent in the appraisal of enjoyment, in the discrimination which crowns the pleasure, finishes it, springing clear and pristine from the turbulence of emotion like that Greek goddess who, I hear, leaped fully-armed from her father's skull? To take in everything — smell, taste, body — with straining senses, with lips, palate and tongue to feel the drops like heavy velvet or crisp silk, pierced by a thousand memories struggling to take form, seized by an intoxication of all the senses that brings forth knowledge: that is a gift granted to few. I inherited it from my father and possess it to such a degree that I can recognize a wine I drank one drop of ten years ago, and name its origin, its vintage.

I was not meant at first to make use of these abilities. My father did not want me to take up his profession, which had yielded him only a meager, hard-earned income. He wanted me to apprentice myself at a trading company that had wide-ranging connections to all the countries in the world and was owned by a distant relative of my mother. The plan foundered on my opposition. I wanted to be a wine-traveler. I easily defeated my father, a kind-hearted man who loved his only child tenderly, by asking whether he would make his son go into the trading company if he were a virtuoso on the violin.

"No," my father said. "Isn't wine like an old violin," I asked, "and isn't it my gift to play this violin like a virtuoso?"

This might lead one to believe that from youth I have been a man of modest ambitions. That I wished to follow my inclinations, finding in them a modest happiness rather than search the wide world for the frenetic activity that is no happiness at all. That I wanted to be nothing but what my father was. Let me say at once that this was not the case. What I write here of the world's frenetic activity, I did not know at the time. I came by this knowledge the hard way. Fate has been a stern teacher to me, sterner perhaps than to many whose lives follow their prescribed paths quietly and without upheaval. Do you suppose that I was not tantalized and tempted by the thought of earning money like my childless uncle, whose fortune I doubtless would have inherited? Money, luxury, the power to pay for women and give them presents, to go through life as a man of distinction — at the time, that must have been my heart's most ardent desire. If I rejected the offer which promised all this for the future, it was because I thought it should all fall into my lap in an easier, more gratifying way, effortlessly, not hard won through honest, respectable work in my uncle's office under his strict supervision. Not only did I believe, I was absolutely convinced there must exist bold, venturesome ways to come into money without the slightest effort. Despite my youth, there was no faith in my heart that honesty, thrift and hard work would always be rewarded. I believed the opposite.

I had no clear notion of how to make good on my dreams. I sensed only that one must be at the ready, free of prejudices, uninhibited, to seize the opportunity when it arose. I thought up all sorts of situations from which I emerged with huge profits.

There is one I remember in particular. I will give myself the benefit of the doubt and suppose that it is especially dear to me because I triumphed less by deception than through my art.

On one of my trips, I thought, I come to a town. It is an insignificant little town, far from the beaten path. A town of whose existence I am unaware until the day I arrive. Some escapade has brought me here. I take a room at the inn, dress, as I generally do, slowly and meticulously, perhaps more slowly than usual to keep the innkeeper in suspense. I know the innkeeper is lying in wait to sound me out. He is as curious as only an innkeeper can be. I go downstairs. I sit at a table. The innkeeper comes to start a conversation with me. I am short of words. Then the wine is brought. The bottle is old and dusty, without a label. I pour a glass full. Bordeaux. Even before I drink I am seized by that seductive unrest, a tremor of the senses as must seize artists when they are suddenly, unexpectedly overcome by the vision of a work. A moment later I crush the first drop between tongue and palate. A voluptuous warmth courses through my blood. I close my eyes. I have before me the most exquisite wine I ever drank. The crowning glory of all wines. A hundred years old for certain, a hundred years sealed in the bottle, a hundred years removed from all the influences of the earth, left to itself, grown ripe, ripe as a tropical fruit, of gentle heft, supple sweetness, fit to flow down the throats of the most discriminating connoisseurs. A second only, and I know everything. I open my eyes. I look at the innkeeper. He has no inkling of my discovery.

To this day I distinctly recall the taste of this wine, although

I never drank it. Its bouquet tickles the nerves of my nose as if I were holding the glass before me now. I know I will never really breathe this fragrance, never feel on my tongue the taste that memory conjures up. Memory? Memory? Memory of something I never really experienced? You will laugh at that. But for me it is no different than a real experience. I find no special feature to distinguish this experience from others. If this is not true, then I was never really a wine-traveler, I only dreamed it, and I no longer know whether I really killed a man or whether it was a dream.

I believe one should not seek to discover what was real in the past and what was not. The thought is strange and disquieting. It is a comfort when the heart makes no distinctions.

I set up the swindle cleverly. I did not mention the wine to the innkeeper that day. When I paid I saw that the innkeeper valued the wine worth thousands at a few pennies. The next day, no sooner, I talked the unsuspecting innkeeper into selling me his entire supply, one hundred and ten bottles, and was a wealthy man.

I was barely eighteen when my father entrusted me with his notebook. This book was my father's scepter. With it he bequeathed me his knowledge of the clientele. It was a little octavo booklet with a dog-eared cardboard cover held together by an elastic cord. The book was small enough to fit, with some difficulty, into one's outside jacket pocket. Opening it, one saw on the right side a flight of white letters on rectangular red fields, A to Z. This book was not used to record customers' orders. For that there were slender notebooks with carbon-paper inserts and a pre-printed text, the sort every traveling salesman has. I doubt, though, that any traveling salesman owns a book like the one my father left me. Over forty years in the trade my father had noted all he deemed important for a salesman in the districts we traveled, characterizations of the people one dealt with, their personalities, their connections, localities, prices — seeing that this list fails to bring the picture to life, I shall quote a few lines from my father's book verbatim.

"M. Red-haired scoundrel. Handle with caution. Complains about every shipment. Drunk by day, come in the evening. O. Nephew of F. in . . . Buy tin of sardines. Give F.'s regards. Ask if leg is hurting again. Rail at the Jews. Good orders, bottled wines. From Meyer & Ludwig. Don't leave."

As these examples show, my father, if not an outstanding man, was at least an outlandish one. Now that I have begun to speak of my father, I cannot resist telling one more thing about him, even if it interrupts the flow of my narrative. But ultimately I am interested not in writing an absorbing story, but in recording my life's crucial particulars. Is it presumptuous of me to think my life important enough to be recorded for posterity? I write neither to edify nor to uplift. I need answer to no one. Perhaps I only want to pass once more in spirit, step by step, down the road I have come, for in the heart's helpless torment there is secret pleasure in the inability to make what happened happen again differently. I will experience the stations of this road again, and in the midst of this experience I will know the inevitable end. Was it inevitable even then, before I knew it? Or could I have taken fate to another end with another word, another decision? O God, let me believe that everything was inevitably ordained for me. Alas, memory is not obliterated, over and over again it seems to confront us with the decision which is an inescapable compulsion, the compulsion to follow a mysterious Before which ultimately never existed either, just as a dream makes you utter panicked words whose sound reverberates in your ears from the past or the future. All things are filled with agonizing mystery where man loses his way.

I meant to speak of my father. I meant to say that he retired with an easy mind, though he had put away barely enough to keep body and soul together. I should not like anyone to think my father a fool after reading what I write about him. The peculiarity I am about to divulge gave his life a quiet happiness. My father had a secret. No one knew it, only he and I, and that filled him with quiet joy. People took him for a poor old wine-traveler and not for what he really was, and he found that so exquisite that he could hardly contain his mirth. My father, you see, was a great statesman. In the year '66* he had saved Austria from defeat through an alliance with Russia. This was proven irrefutably by the papers hidden away in his desk from curious eyes. As was many another diplomatic deed that had had the most profound influence upon Europe's political constellation. His alliances, military campaigns and peace treaties had had a broader and more salutary significance than those one reads of in the papers, for which my father could spare only an ironic smile.

My father often explained to me the fundamental political principles he had followed in all his combinations, campaigns, alliances and secret treaties. The statesman, he would say, stroking his sparse white beard, must have his own view of the world, and he must not let himself be swayed from his path by accounts others give him. In contrast to all my other contemporaries whom the world sees fit to call statesmen, I have always drawn upon my own resources and never relied on tale-bearers, be they newspapermen or diplomats. My worldview was that of a peace-loving, enlightened man who understood the plight of the people. I managed to steer clear of great wars into which others plunged headlong, and I believe I acted rightly, even when I enjoyed the support of strong confederates and could predict a victory with almost mathematical certainty. I was ever conscious of the grave responsibility that God had vested in me, and I believe I need not accuse myself of abusing it. I can die at peace and go before the heavenly judge who will weigh my deeds and those of other statesmen. I need not tremble at the verdict.

So my father spoke to me at times when we were alone. Around others he was not a statesman, but a retired small-time wine-traveler who discussed the prospects for the harvest and the untenable price increases in recent years. As I mentioned, he saw it as an amusing prank he played on the world by concealing his true works, a little roguery he indulged in for his and my pleasure, making him burst out in a child's mischievous laughter whenever we spoke of it. I imagine he felt like the ruler in the fairy tale who mingled with his subjects incognito and joined their conversations, blissful in his subterfuge, a secret caliph like my father.

At the time, so as not to disappoint the old man, I pretended to listen gravely and agree with him, but I often laughed at him myself. Today I laugh no longer. Aren't we all secret caliphs? We all build ourselves the house of our life, and the world around us sees it differently. Why do we let others delude us into seeing our life with their eyes? Better to smile at them like my father, for not knowing what we know, instead of believing them. If we think up our future, why not do the same with the past — what is the difference between past and future? — and be secret caliphs like Harun al-Rashid?* The common folk say: If they call you a cow, you have to moo. Who is right, those people or my father?

I shall not dwell on these questions, seeing that learned men have doubtless explained and answered them in their books long ago, and I would only lose my way in a labyrinth of doubts. I shall now start telling the story I should already have begun with rather than letting myself digress.

After taking over my father's business, I began by calling on the clients whom he himself had visited several times a year over the decades. Going by my father's notebook, I introduced myself to each as the son of my father, followed my father's written instructions, spoke with one of his gout, with another of his daughter in Vienna, and had no cause for complaint. Business went tolerably well. I sold enough to live modestly and save a few pennies here and there for my old age. Yet I was not content with these prospects. I had not gone into this profession only to practice it as my father had. There was no doubt in my mind that mine was a different, richer fate. The knowledge of the great talent I possessed, that unearned gift of nature, led me to demand more of life than had yet been granted me, rather than to acquire it patiently through perseverance and hard work. In my presumption, I never doubted that everything else must follow just as effortlessly upon this talent, as if to make my life's outward circumstances worthy of my art.

The first money I came by I invested in clothes, cravats, shoes and walking sticks. Elegance, the fine gentleman's air, that, I thought, is the secret of being a fine gentleman. Can a man be a success in life if his external appearance relegates him from the outset to the failures, the little people, those who life has driven to the wall? Petty fates are no less contagious than misfortune. How could my father have achieved a lofty fate, associating as he did only with provincial innkeepers, riding the railway third class, wearing ten-year-old clothes and agonizing over every penny he spent! Why should luck have smiled upon him, out of all the masses of little people? Luck must be met halfway. If you are young and slender as I, with a handsome face, sporting good clothes and the manner of one whom luck has singled out, then the great adventure will come to sweep you away. Perhaps it's a beautiful, wealthy woman you meet on the train or in the lobby of a grand hotel, perhaps a big industrialist who spots you, captivated by your acumen, your assurance, your pleasing appearance. And indeed you are fanciful enough to grasp and use the opportunity the moment it presents itself. You have a right to wait for this destiny, to seize it reckless and uninhibited when it's there, for you are richer than others, chosen by God for a special fate, you are an artist in a different sphere than the poet or the musician, but like them raised by your senses into a deeper and holier communion with Nature, lifted up from the inert masses of those whose eyes are as dull as their ears, their nostrils, their tongues, and the nerves beneath their skin.

I meant to earn only the first of my money in my father's profession. Then away from home, first to the capital, then traveling all the countries on earth. Back then, when I sat evenings in a small-town inn after a day's work, drinking a bottle of cheap wine, I vividly beheld my life as it would shortly be. I felt on my tongue the fiery, heady wine I would drink, swooning in the grip of the pleasure that was my due. I was surrounded by rich young men and beautiful women I drew after me into the beatitude of pleasure. They had never drunk like this before. I revealed to them the mystery of the wine we drank. In old wine is the scent of all flowers, the rays of the sun, children's laughter, men's sweat, the vision of the summer landscape, all ripe and heavy as the breast of a nursing mother. I did not reveal it in words, my senses revealed it, as women's mute sensuality reveals itself and plunges into sweet transport.

My father's customers began to regard me with suspicion. The small-time innkeepers and tradesmen took it as an affront when a salesman came to tout his wines wearing slender patent-leather boots and fashionable cravats. What they admired in their social superiors, they resented in me. It was presumptuous of me to dress better than they. Was I more than they, or wasn't I actually less, weren't they the buyers, and didn't I have to be happy and say thank you when they ordered a few bottles of cheap Vöslauer? They stopped placing orders with me. I'd see how far I got with my gentlemanly elegance, lording it over them.

And so I did not find it hard to leave my cramped sphere of activity after a year and go to the capital, which I had visited several times. Here I would take my first steps into life's wide arena and then move on into the wide world, many parts of which I knew as if I had already beheld them. I knew the sight of Burgundy, and the land of Bordeaux. Wasn't the one a sun-warmed plain and the other a chain of hills on which the snow melts in the earth's warm breath? Could it be otherwise? I knew them all, the red burgundies from Chambertin to Maçon, the whites of Montrachet and Chablis, the red Bordeaux of Médoc, Latour, Chateau Margaux, the whites of Sauterne.

I arrived in the city with money enough to live frugally for several months. But frugality was far from my mind. I took a good room in a pension where travelers stayed, I ate at fashionable restaurants and spent my evenings in the side room of a café where people gambled for high stakes. I wanted my fate to be decided. I did not join in the game. All I wanted at first was to make acquaintances in these circles, to meet people who could be helpful. There could be no more propitious company than that of gamblers. Their money burns a hole in their pocket; they are generous and extravagant when they win; they are easily fired up for foolhardy ideas so long as they harbor the slightest hope of great profits. They believe in the luck that can be forced, they believe the lucky man and shun the man dogged by ill-luck as if he were a criminal.

I met men here who possessed great wealth. Or perhaps they had already squandered it in the blissful hope of increasing it tenfold. My sharp eyes immediately distinguished those men from my kind, the dandies with their seeming indifference toward loss and gain, who like me had nothing to stake but their hunger for money. There was one, a young man, slender, black-haired, always laughing and cracking jokes that made others laugh, dressed with fastidious elegance, airily, heedlessly nonchalant in his movements. Next to him I felt like a greenhorn. Like all the rest he sat in the warm, smoky room in his shirtsleeves, but he never lost his poise. He looked no less consummate in his shirtsleeves than he would have were he wearing evening dress. His elegance was not the breeding of those born to money, not the habituation, the imitation of those who have come into money, it was what mine was, an inner experience of its own, no matter whether one is sitting in one's shirtsleeves at the gaming table or leading a lady onto the dance floor of a ballroom. His name was Wäger. It was said he was about to become engaged to a very rich young woman, a widow. He had brilliant eyes doubtless capable of seducing women. I saw my own desires burning in them. That was how I knew him.

Around two in the morning I would leave the gambling hall. I walked down the narrow city streets to my pension, situated in a new building in the Old Town. Day after day I hoped to meet a woman at the front door or on the stairs, perhaps a foreigner lodging in the pension for a few days. I knew how I would speak to her, how my reserve — nonetheless conveying keen, irresistible desire — would win her over, this very night. How

I would set out with her, perhaps the very next day, not yet at my goal, but already a good deal closer. I never met a woman on the stairs. When I walked down the corridor past strangers' doors to my door, the flicker of the match showed me men's sturdy shoes standing next to women's dainty boots. Sometimes, too, a lonely pair of women's shoes stood outside a door. I would dream of that door while drinking my customary bottle of wine in my room before going to bed. I get up, open the door where the women's shoes stand, a frightened woman cries out, I grope for the light, I ask her to be still, I tell her that I want only an hour with her, that I had no choice but to break in on her at the risk of her rousing the house, summoning the police to arrest me like a criminal. And I do not return to my room that night, not until the first footsteps wake in the house do I slip away from her, who has me swear a thousand times over that I love her and will never leave her. She is rich, her pearls alone are worth more than a fair-sized vineyard. I have money, enough to go to Monte, break the bank and restore her possessions with a casual gesture.

When I think back upon this time today, I break in on this woman and my life takes a different course than it took. Back then I did not do it. Did I lack faith in my luck after all, did I fear the truth, did my heart, sated by these dreams, no longer desire the deed? Was it my father's legacy within me, mistaking fantasy for reality? Reality! Thinking back, would it have been more real to break into that unknown woman's room than to live it out panting in my heart? Dreams like these left me happily exhausted all night long, without desire. I no longer had the strength to act. Perhaps deep down in my heart, barely known to me, there was a doubt that stopped the deed. The doubt whether acting still mattered when the act had already been thus experienced. I believe it may be impossible to be both a real victor and a secret one.

When I saw that my money was running low, I began to gamble. I avoided sitting at the table where Wäger sat; I feared our fates might be in each other's way. Sometimes I won small amounts, only to lose them again. One day I wagered my last gold piece. Sacrifice the last you have, don't be petty, stake everything on one card, that reconciles fate, that forces luck! I lost. Fate wants further sacrifices, I thought. That was not enough. I have a watch in my pocket. I inherited it from my father. His wedding present from my mother. An old watch that has to be wound with a little key. But gold all the same. Fate smiles upon him who, free of petty sentimental inhibitions, sells it his heart, as people once sold themselves to the devil.

The waiter gave me a few silver coins. I returned to the gambling hall. My eyes met Wäger's. I smiled. I went up to the table, again I staked everything on one card. I won. I left my winnings where they were, I won again. Three times in a row I won this way. People began to take notice of me. Gambling halls fall still in such moments. All that is heard is the voice of the croupier. Everyone seems to sense that a fate is in the balance. I staked all my winnings a fourth and fifth time and won again. Then I decided to withdraw half of what I had won. The cards fell. I had lost.

The excitement ebbed from the hall. The babble of voices

reached my ears again like the roar of falling water from a distance. I understood what had happened. Luck had turned its back on me when I doubted it, when I tried to make a cautious pact with it, when the petty-bourgeois wine-traveler woke within me. I would wrest it back. I took the rest of my money and staked it. A few seconds later my fate was decided. I had lost.

I stood up and looked around me. I sought Wäger's eyes. He was the only person who could help me. To him I could admit that I was at the end of my rope. For one moment Wäger looked at me. His gaze seemed hostile. As if to say: We are not confederates, you're mistaken. I have luck and you do not. Don't cling to me, go, I say, go!

I went. Should I go home? Tomorrow morning I would have to pay the past week's rent. I would find some excuse and leave the house. I had my words at the ready. But then, what then? I didn't know anyone in the city well enough to count on their assistance. I couldn't sell my suits without abandoning all hope of traveling in the moneyed classes. All that remained were fantastic hopes of an extraordinary stroke of luck that would put money into my hands tomorrow. To go to a wine-merchant and sell him so much wine that the profit would keep my head above water a while longer. I forgot that I was ignorant of the latest prices and had no idea what the companies I represented had in stock, and that a merchant could not be expected to immediately place a large order with a stranger like me. As I made these plans, my desperation subsided.

Without realizing it, I was not taking the shortest route home. I was walking slowly along the quay. I did not meet a soul. It was three in the morning, a warm June night. I sat on a bench. The murmur of water in its regularity soothed me like the view of the dark mass of hills on the opposite bank. I made out the silhouette of the castle standing out sharply against the sky. I heard steps. A woman was approaching. She would have to walk right past me. In the first dull glimmer of morning I saw that she wore a hat and a wrap, perhaps a fur.

When she was about five steps away from my bench, I made a movement. She flinched, halted, and seemed to consider whether she shouldn't turn around and make a little detour. Suddenly cheerful, I laughed. "Don't be afraid," I said, "don't be afraid. I'm glad enough to be left alone myself."

I rose to my feet. Inspecting my suit, she regained her composure.

"Oh," she said, "I . . . Sometimes homeless people sleep on these benches here."

"I could be homeless too."

I came closer. I saw that she was a young, pretty girl, but certainly not the one I was waiting for. It amused me to think that we were both seeking our fortune in similar ways, each hoping at this moment to find it in the other.

"Homeless," she said, "you!" She looked at me incredulously. Why put on an act in front of her, I thought. I'll tell her. Everything is easier in the telling.

"Tonight," I said, "I gambled away everything. Even my father's golden watch. It was a wedding present from my mother."

"Oh God, you shouldn't have done that. That was bad luck."

"I can't go back to my hotel. How am I supposed to pay the rent tomorrow? You see — I don't know where I'm going to sleep tonight."

"I'll take you with me," she said.

"I mean it, I don't have any money."

"No, no, not for money. There's a hotel over on that side street. They know me there. I'll pay for the room. I'll take you along, just like that, for fun. And you . . . you'll have money again some day, sure enough!"

"Agreed," I said.

I liked her. She was slender, blonde, with nice teeth and thin lips. And she spoke so decidedly that there was no room for contradiction. Hardly waiting for my reply, she took me by the arm and led the way.

Crossing the little square with the memorial to an emperor, we turned off into a narrow, dark, ill-paved street. In front of a derelict house we stopped. She rang. Above us hung an extinguished lantern with the red lettering: Hotel.

We heard steps inside. A scantily dressed girl about seventeen years old, red-haired, with tiny eyes and a bloodless face, opened the door for us. With one skinny arm she lit the way up the stairs to a small room containing a rumpled bed, a bedside table with a candle, and a sofa covered with a filthy sheet.

"Tidy up the room," I said to the girl. "Never mind," said Lili, "she's weak in the head." Lili tidied up the room herself. "Do you want anything," she asked, "to eat, to drink?"

"Wine," I said.

"And you shall have it!" Her gesture was that of a king bestowing a province. She went downstairs. Below I heard her voice, waking the innkeeper and asking him to hurry. I heard a door open, and shuffling steps, as of swollen, gouty feet in slippers. My breath catches when I think back on that moment. I feel as if something within me took fathomless fright at the sound. Did an awful memory wake dark and mysterious in my heart? Or does our blood curdle when the unknown, soon to be our fate, first brushes the edge of our existence? I sprang up and hurried to the door. I wanted to flee. A hideous fear had seized me.

Lili returned with the wine, laughing. She saw me standing in the doorway with my hat on my head. She gave me a startled, questioning look. I felt I could not refuse the generosity she delighted in without explaining everything. I was about to speak. But already all my fear dissolved. I laughed. I was ashamed of my groundless fright. Oh, if only I had followed my first impulse and fled! If it is possible to flee one's fate, I would have escaped an awful one, now but a few hours off.

We drank a dry Mosel wine, better than I had hoped. Lili enjoyed playing hostess. I let her tend to me like a child. We drank, chatted, laughed and went to bed. Soon Lili fell asleep, one last happy smile playing about her lips. I did not sleep. I was filled with tense inner unrest for which I knew no reason but the excitement of the game still trembling within me. I believe everyone knows this alertness of the aroused senses which intensifies from one minute to the next, and only increases with the growing weariness of the body, the almost aching slackness of the limbs. You want to jump out of bed, bolt across the room and out into the street. You strain with an inexplicable agitation. Suddenly you feel the urge to sing, to wail like a child too tired to fall asleep.

I lay like that until what must have been noon in the room's curtained darkness. Then I succumbed to a restless slumber, tormented by wild dreams. I played the same game I had played that evening, but the cards fell differently. They fell for me. I played against a fat man who sat facing me. I felt that this man was completely soft, without bones. I won, but my pile of money dwindled and dwindled, while the shapeless fat man's grew. He smiled, I would have flown into a rage, but I could not move, could hardly breathe, a greasy, shapeless, disgustingly soft mass weighed upon me. A noise woke me. Lili was washing. It was late in the afternoon. She hurried off. She put money on the table for me to pay the innkeeper. Ashamed of yesterday's whim, Lili took care of the business with the brisk ill-temper she knew from her customers. The thought made me smile. She said "Goodbye" and gave me her hand. I stayed in bed. I had a heavy head.

A knock came at the door. "Who's there?" I called. I heard a soft titter and light footsteps moving away. The halfwit, I thought, the one who lighted our way up the stairs yesterday. I got up. There was money lying on the table. I put it in my pocket. Then I was seized by the impulse to take it out of my pocket again and spit on it. That's what you do with money like that, I thought, and laughed. I laughed, yet already I was marked as the instrument of death and destruction.

I groped my way down the murky, creaking stairway. I

found myself in a dark, flagstoned vestibule, scantly lit by the half-opened front door. A few paces ahead of me I saw the silhouette of a big man without a jacket. His shirt glimmered white.

"Three-fifty," said the innkeeper. The tone of it enraged me as much as his voice. It was a fat falsetto.

"I want something to eat," I said. I must have wanted to play the master giving the orders. He pushed open a door behind me. The halfwit lit the light in a small room whose one side was taken up by a bar. I took a seat. The bare table was coated with filth. Paint had peeled from the walls in places. From the floorboards came the musty smell of decay.

I had the innkeeper bring me a bottle of wine. I ate a piece of hard, juiceless meat and drank. The innkeeper sat facing me. He never took his eyes off me, I could feel it. I thought of starting a conversation, but could not think of a word to say to him. He sat there unmoving, wheezing as he breathed. The noise filled me with unspeakable revulsion. I looked at him, I willed him with my gaze to get up and leave me. He had tiny eyes with fat pouches. His moustache, dirty yellow, hung into his mouth; his head was bald. He had a growth on the back of his head. I could not determine whether it was a boil or a tubercle. I reached into my pocket as if searching for a weapon, and felt the money.

At that moment a thought flashed through my mind. It frightened me at first, but it refused to let me go. Here in my pocket was the chance to force my luck. Hadn't I dreamed I would win? The cards would favor me today, everything would fall into my lap. Luck demands strength. I couldn't let myself be beaten. I wanted money, money, with these bills in my pocket I would win it. It was lucky money, wasn't it? The tables had turned, luck was smiling on me, why else would I have met Lili? How clever of me to spit on it, what an inspiration! It was my last chance, my last salvation. If I disregarded it, wouldn't that mean thrusting luck away, abandoning all I had dreamed of? Here was the fate I had been waiting for. I only had to be strong enough to seize it. I felt that all would be won merely by entering the gambling hall with these bills in my pocket. So firm was my faith.

I did not know how much I had in my pocket. I had not counted it. That, too, was propitious. I would wager it with my eyes closed. Maybe it wouldn't even be enough to satisfy the innkeeper. There would be a scene one way or the other. Was I supposed to waive my claim to luck just because of this fat colossus facing me? Surely he had money enough, in the bank or hidden in his house somewhere. You could tell by looking at him. Pity was uncalled-for. This was the last chance! If I sold a suit tomorrow, I'd have to pay for the rooms. I would need the rest for a meal. Tomorrow I will have eaten nothing for an entire day, I thought. What could I wager then? And will luck be on my side tomorrow? It was my last chance. I had to use it at all costs.

All these thoughts crossed my mind at once, not one by one, but side by side. I had rapidly drained the bottle of wine. I felt free and careless. Tomorrow I would come back and pay the innkeeper, but today I had to leave this place with Lili's money, my luck was at stake. My plan was made. I would find some pretext to get the innkeeper out of the room and seize the chance to make my getaway. I called to him for a new bottle of wine. He got up and shuffled out of the room. Just as I was about to jump to my feet, the door opened. The halfwit came in and stood by the door.

It was clear to me that she was following orders. I could have risen, gone to the door and shoved her out of the way. That struck me as risky. If the innkeeper returned before I was out the door, while I was busy with the halfwit, my escape would be thwarted. So I decided to lure the halfwit over to me while I still sat there innocently, and then, when she came up, give her a shove to keep her from stopping me and leave the house in one bound.

I called to her. "You! Come here!" She gave me an empty animal look. She wore a white, long-unwashed, sleeveless jacket of coarse linen which hung loose over her short skirt. Her legs were bare as her feet and thin as her arms. Her face had a corpse-like pallor, as if it had never seen the sun. Her cheekbones spread wide, making her face flatter and more expressionless than it already was. Either her greasy red hair was thinning, or she had never had more than enough for the five-inch braid which stood out stiff as a rod from the back of her head. I rapped on the table, waved my glass at her. She seemed to understand and came closer, dangling her hands flat and rigid in front of her body and tilting back her head so that her face turned upward. She moved forward like the figures in the weather boxes the farmers hang in their windows.

When she stood next to me, I poised to jump up. She had

left the door open. Then the innkeeper loomed in the door with the wine bottle. I had half risen to my feet. Pretending I had been joking with the halfwit, I thumped her on the back.

"Hahaha," shrieked the innkeeper, "you like her, hahaha!"

"She's your daughter?"

"My only, darling child, hahaha!"

Hearing her father laughing, the only child laughed along. It sounded hideous, like the gurgling sound some people make when they drink. The old man stopped laughing. He looked at his daughter angrily. The halfwit took a step toward the wall and cringed like a dog.

"Laughing," cried the innkeeper, "laughing . . . you . . ."

She tried to slip past along the wall. He grabbed her by the stiff little braid, pulled her up and punched her in the face. The halfwit child gasped faintly, and when he let her go she tumbled to the ground. The struck cheek was dark red. The halfwit rose and staggered from the room.

"What are you doing?" I cried.

"What am I doing? I gave her a good smack, in case you didn't notice. That's a good one, sir!"

He sat down again heavily. I quickly poured myself a glass of wine and emptied it in one gulp. In my pocket I felt the money. I thought of nothing but escaping the innkeeper.

I have written down the story of my life. No doubt I may have dwelt too long on superfluous details. But I have intentionally withheld nothing in my earlier life which could serve to explain what happened now. Today, I believe, I view myself calmly and coolly. I see all that was evil in me, and I wish to extenuate nothing. And yet: I have no explanation for what I did in that moment. Do people's actions follow a law? Where is it? Was I the tool of a higher will? Why me? Alas, one step follows another by a secret law that leaves no choice, you can move your foot forward, but never backward, and in the end a man's first breath is his life's inevitable destiny!

I planned if need be to slip past the innkeeper with my money. I set myself a time to jump up. The bottle was half empty. When it is empty, let it be done. Outside the first guests were arriving. The halfwit led them up the stairs to a room. It was time. I would drain the last glass to the dregs and hurl it to the ground. Taking advantage of the innkeeper's confusion, I would bolt past him. I drank slowly, as if dreading the moment I had chosen to act. I did not look at the innkeeper. I felt his gaze upon me and heard his rhythmic wheezing.

The door opened, and the halfwit came in. Her cheek had swollen up until one eye showed only as a narrow slit. She went behind the bar. I heard the jingle of keys. At once I understood. I had not reckoned with that. I rose to my feet. I sensed that it must be done now, in a minute the front door would be locked. It is inexplicable that I did not bolt forward at once, as I had planned. The innkeeper had risen as well. He looked at me. I felt that he was sneering. Suddenly I remembered the soft mass which had weighed upon me in my dream. I seized my hat and took a few uncertain steps forward.

The innkeeper blocked my path. "Little brother, little brother," he said. I remember these words distinctly. It is inexplicable what frightened me about them.

He poked me in the chest with one outstretched finger. I staggered back against the table. My left hand was in my pocket, clutching the money meant to save me. My right hand rested on the table behind me. Suddenly I heard a cry I myself had uttered. The innkeeper moved toward me. I heard the shuffle of his slippers. I felt as if a shapeless dough were moving in on me, about to envelop me. I leaned back over the table. My hand grasped something hard, cold. Now he was only a step away from me. I felt he was about to say something else, perhaps "little brother." Anything, anything but that! I had to get away! I brought the hard thing down on his skull. The bottle rolled onto the floor. It did not break. A good wine bottle, I thought. The innkeeper stopped in his tracks. He did not move. Why isn't he coming, I thought, why isn't he coming? I don't know how long we both stood there motionless. Suddenly he fell to his knees. Then his body toppled over, face down. It sounded heavy and hollow, like a sack of flour hitting the ground.

The halfwit walked up, squatted next to the corpse and gurgled.

The inquiry concluded that the halfwit had murdered her father in a fit of bestial vengeance. She was committed to a lunatic asylum.

I signed a lease with the owner of the house and took the dead man's place as innkeeper. I did so because I had no other prospects at the moment. Besides, I tried to convince myself that rejecting the offer might cast suspicion upon me. Perhaps the real reason was that I found it hard to leave this place. Fate charged me, as it were, to carry on the life of the innkeeper.

Now I take the guests to their rooms at night and lie in wait for my money in the vestibule. I invest it not in clothes now, but in old wines.

I flee memory with its torment of the irretrievable decision. At night I have no time to think. In the morning I sleep. In the afternoon business is slow. I do as the artists do. As they flee conscience in their dreams, so do I. I fetch a bottle of wine and drink. I drink the way others listen to music. In these hours I live my life over again, and I decide differently. One time I go into my uncle's business, one time I remain a wine-traveler, or I do not change my path until the day I sold my father's watch. I play differently, win and go to my hotel. If the innkeeper is dead anyway, then it really was the halfwit who killed him. Or Wäger lends me money. I say one little word to Lili: No. And happiness, respect, success are mine. In the end it seems to me the past isn't irrevocable after all. I smile as my father smiled when he spoke of his diplomatic triumphs. No one knows about it, and that is what's so exquisite! I walk through Baghdad incognito as the caliph.

REASONS FOR EVERYTHING

Leopold stood outside the door of the building he had just left, thinking. He felt that he had forgotten something upstairs. He turned slowly and climbed back up the three steep flights of stairs to the musician.

"I beg your pardon," he said and walked inside.

He saw the picture as soon as he entered the room. He had only glanced at it before. And now he knew that what he had forgotten was the memory of the picture.

"A remarkable picture," he said, looking at it in consternation. "Really a most remarkable picture."

"Yes," said the musician. He was surprised that Leopold had nothing else to say.

Leopold turned at the door.

"I'm going to Wilhelm Rau's tavern on Brunnenstrasse. You know the tavern. I'll be there until ten o'clock. After that I'll go home."

The musician did not ask: Why are you telling me this?

He was a diffident young musician.

The thought of the picture was hard for Leopold. It was a picture in a simple frame. It showed a tabletop. A man with bony hands outspread over the tabletop was counting silver pieces. The hands were thin and the fingers long. Next to him sat a woman with sagging breasts shown rather than hidden by a loose smock. She, too, had outspread hands. Liquid was spilled on the table, apparently a sticky liquid. The faces were angular, white and severe. They were bony faces, thin, suffering and outspread like the hands.

Leopold thought this picture could be called "Communion" or "The Host." It called to mind things it probably had nothing to do with, any more than it had to do with communion. At bottom it was a worldly picture. It was the hands that made it sacred, and the eyes.

The hands were outspread. That was the amazing thing. Leopold had never heard the word that way before. But it was a familiar sacred word. Maybe it came from a forgotten hymn.

The musician began to play. Leopold heard it because the musician's window was open wide. The street was deserted.

He remembered that he had promised the musician to go to Brunnenstrasse. The musician might come looking for him. It was nine o'clock.

Leopold struck up a brisk pace.

The thought of the picture was hard. Now Leopold felt that the liquid spilled on the table was not wine or liquor, as he had thought at first, but blood. Though the picture had made it seem that black and white were the only colors, the damp stain on the table looked red, sticky and not yet dry. With his fingers he felt distinctly that it was nothing like liquor or wine to the touch, that the stickiness was not from sugar, it was the viscosity of blood. It seemed to have drained from the bloodless fingers. But perhaps it was there from earlier. The barkeeper, coming to wipe it from the table, drew back; Leopold did not move his fingers away from it, leaving his beer untouched and looking at the barkeeper coldly.

There was no doubt that it would all be cleared up shortly: when the musician who owned the picture came. He would be able to say what all this was.

Leopold straightened up, and his elbows moved away from his body. But he kept his fingers outspread. Alarmed at the blood on the table, he looked at the door, the door had to open. There was no one in the room but the barkeeper.

Leopold rubbed his forehead. For the thought of the picture was hard. He wanted to forget the thought.

But the money, he thought. What about the money? There are reasons for everything.

"Reasons," he said aloud, and the word seemed unfathomable, strange and almost unendurable.

He left without drinking his beer. He thought of all the money it cost and how his wife went hungry. But he had promised the musician. And now he had not come.

It struck ten as he came out onto the street. He began to walk.

His wife sat in the room in a smock. He saw her sagging breasts, shown more than hidden by the smock. It hadn't been a month since the baby died.

Leopold took the money from his pocket and laid it on the table in front of his wife. It was six silver pieces the musician had given him for taking notation.

There was a smell of fresh meat. The meat lay in a bowl by the window.

"Moritz?" asked Leopold.

Moritz, the black cat was called.

He took the meat from the bowl and brought it and laid it on the tabletop.

"Let's eat," he said.

They ate and tossed the bones into the corner. Nothing was left of Moritz but a damp stain on the table. They sat side by side.

"Soon guests will come," he said.

They waited for the musician.

Toward morning her smock fell open, and her breasts, the breasts he knew, sagged over the table. They were poor, empty breasts. They were severe and outspread.

When she was still nursing the baby, blood flowed from her breasts instead of milk. He looked at the breasts. There was a horrible stain on the table.

The blood killed the baby, he thought.

They're lovely breasts, he thought, outspread empty breasts. Do they still ooze blood? Onto the smock? In the end the smock will turn out to be caked with blood. These are hard thoughts to think, these are hard thoughts.

Maybe, thought Leopold, when the musician comes and sees this, the breasts, the stain, the money and the smock, the dear empty bleeding breasts, maybe he can tell us the reasons for everything. They are there. But unfathomable, strange and almost unendurable. Leopold, O Leopold.

TULPE

Senior File Clerk Tulpe died at 10 in the morning. He had entered Room 47 at eight in the morning as always, cheerfully returned the greeting of File Clerk Kleinmeyer, already at his place, and taken his seat. As always, Tulpe had first undone the bottom two buttons of his vest, which stretched over his paunch when he sat, then brushed his moustache and his long forked beard, and lit his cigar. After a brief exchange with Kleinmeyer about the poor prospects for that year's harvest, he had taken his breakfast bread-and-butter out of his briefcase, divided it into four parts with his pocket knife, painstakingly wrapped three pieces back up in the paper and locked them in his desk drawer, while beginning to chew slowly and elaborately on the fourth part. File Clerk Kleinmeyer noticed nothing out of the ordinary. Punctually at nine-thirty Senior File Clerk Tulpe rose from his seat and, as always at this time, took the key with the big wooden block that hung on the wall next to the door, and went to answer the call of nature.

File Clerk Kleinmeyer continued with his breakfast unsuspecting. By unwritten agreement, at ten on the dot it was File Clerk Kleinmeyer's turn to accept the key from Senior File Clerk Tulpe. In all the fifteen years Tulpe and Kleinmeyer had sat across from each other this agreement had been scrupulously observed. Both, Tulpe and Kleinmeyer alike, were men of order.

That Tulpe, as the senior in rank, had the right to the key in the morning before Kleinmeyer was so self-evident to both that neither Tulpe nor Kleinmeyer could ever have entertained the notion of reversing this order. On the other hand, it seemed equally self-evident that at a certain point in time Kleinmeyer must come into his right as well. Senior File Clerk Tulpe having failed to return to the room by four minutes past ten, Kleinmeyer rose, inevitably concerned by Tulpe's unpunctuality. Such an irregularity on Tulpe's part had never occurred before. A delay en route was highly unlikely, for Tulpe knew how very much Kleinmeyer, through fifteen years of habituation, had come to rely upon the punctual transfer of the key.

Greatly alarmed, Kleinmeyer left the room and knocked on the door behind which Tulpe must have locked himself. Hearing no response and fearing the worst, he alerted several gentlemen. The door was forced open, and entering the room they saw Senior File Clerk Tulpe lying lifeless on the floor, incompletely clothed, his massive body, after nearly twenty-five years of service, wedged into the cramped space between wall and plumbing.

No doubt about it, death had taken Senior File Clerk Tulpe unawares. Not only did an embarrassing clothing deficiency indicate as much, a Second Class Assistant reported that he had met the Senior File Clerk on his last walk, cheerfully swinging the key and contentedly humming the song "What Good's My Rose Garden to Me?" as he hastened to his destination. Had Senior File Clerk Tulpe anticipated what awaited him, he would presumably have taken pains to be surprised by death in a more seemly position, given his pronounced feeling for the dignity and prestige of his office.

As soon as the death became known, a conference was held in the director's office. In brief, pithy words the director eulogized the man carried off so abruptly in the midst of his duties, a man of whom one could rightly say that he died with his boots on. At the same time the director admonished the gentlemen of the department to divulge no details of the death, out of consideration for the venerable tradition of Filing Department B 23.

In the meantime, the deeply moved File Clerk Kleinmeyer had restored the clothing of the Senior File Clerk to its prescribed order and laid out the corpse of his deceased friend on several chairs in the corridor. Then Tulpe was loaded into a hackney cab and brought home by Kleinmeyer, who was to break the news to the widow and render consolation. The thought that the man who lay dead beside him in the hackney cab, who had worn a beard like Kleinmeyer himself, that the man with whom, for fifteen years, he had consumed his breakfast in tandem and used the same place to relieve himself, that this estimable, orderly public servant not only had to die, but had died in a way disgraceful to his position, brought tears to Kleinmeyer's eyes. They were still trickling into his beard when Kleinmeyer stood before Mrs. or rather Widow Senior File Clerk Tulpe. It was hard to comfort the poor woman. Kleinmeyer pointed out that Tulpe had been swept away in the midst of his beloved occupation. He recalled the melancholy song which, to all appearances, Tulpe had had upon his lips when he died. But Mrs. Tulpe called to mind all her husband's little ways, and each time a torrent of tears burst forth from a bosom surging with inner devastation. She enumerated all the dear little traits of the deceased: that he preferred Swiss cheese to Harz, that great and distinguished character; that he exhorted passersby to discipline in his strong voice, ordering this person to walk to the right or the left, that person not to dawdle or to be quicker about getting off the streetcar; that he had found opportunity to scold the neighbors, be it that they trod too loudly, be it that they banged their doors, that outstanding citizen whose achievements as a private man came to life before Kleinmeyer in the widow's stories.

"This plate of cheese," said Widow Tulpe, taking the plate out of the cupboard, "I fixed it for Tulpe for his supper. What good's his rose garden to him . . ." and her voice choked with tears.

Meanwhile Kleinmeyer wondered whether this would be a good time to ask the widow for Tulpe's top hat for the day of the funeral. On that day all the gentlemen in the department would need their top hats themselves, except for Tulpe. Tulpe and Kleinmeyer had the same shape of head. Surely Tulpe's top hat would fit him. But the widow went on to describe how he had made his own sandwiches — in her emotion she called him, for the first time, the dear departed — and how he had refused to entrust anyone else with the job. And so Kleinmeyer was unable to find a proper opening. He took his leave from the Senior File Clerk's widow and postponed his undertaking until the following day. He left the apartment in the uplifting consciousness of possessing a fine sense of propriety.

ALEXANDER

A Fragment

I am called Alexander, and for us that is a curious and unusual name. The other boys were called Josef, Franz, Wenzel, Ladislav. Only I had this special name: I believe the name was the cause of it all. Had I been called Prokop or Cyril, I, too, would have stayed home and become a farmer, a craftsman, a hired hand, or even a pastor like Josef Chlup. True, Wenzel Svatek hanged himself, and I was the one who found him dangling from a slender sapling in the copse. He was fourteen years old. But that had reasons of its own, and I did not mean to go into them.

I would have liked to be called Anton like my father. But more than that I would have liked to be called Cyril or Methodius like our patron saints whose brightly-painted statue stands at the entrance to the village. I remember that statue vividly, though it's twenty years now since I saw it last. The two saints stand side by side, one holding the cross in his hand, the other the Bible. It's as if they're passing through our town. On their holiday the saints' statue is wreathed with garlands. I thought it must be a fine thing to have a name day that's a holiday for all, a day when no one has to go to school.

I was reminded of all this today when the master sat in the music room with his son to listen to the young lady of the house. The young lady played the piano. She is sixteen years old, the master's daughter. No guests were there, she played for pleasure. That made me think of our Jew. He was the son of the town shopkeeper. We were in the same class, though he was younger than I, because the school had only two classes, and in each one different years, girls and boys, all studied together. It wasn't that the Jew was always well-dressed. The postmaster's son also wore shoes on his feet, even in the summer. But the son of the Jew went to a teacher in the afternoons with a music-book under his arm and took piano lessons. None of us took piano lessons. There were wealthy farmers' sons among us and sons of civil servants. But no one went to a teacher to learn how to play the piano. I hated the Jew very much. It seems to me that I hated him so much precisely because he was the only one to go to a teacher in the afternoon with a music-book under his arm, to play the piano for pleasure alone and for no other reason.

I know that is not a satisfactory explanation. But I have no better. When I think of our Jew, even today, I always see him hurrying off to school to see the teacher in little black boots and a blue suit with the music-book under his arm, even though I saw him every day in many other situations. I tell myself how absurd it is to hate a person for such a foolish reason. But even today the blood rises to my head, and I clench my fists in my pockets at the memory.

My father worked for the Jew's father, unloading sacks of spices and boxes of sugar from the wagons and hauling them to the storeroom, a large, dark, flagstoned room lit by three narrow loopholes under the roof. I often helped my father, for though still a boy I had great physical strength. My father was a big, hot-tempered man, and he cursed at the sight of me. Often he would throw a heavy stone at me, or some piece of iron that happened to be at hand. When he got angry the veins swelled on his forehead, and the little vessels that shot the whites of his eyes turned blood-red. I had to watch my step when I worked with him. When the master, the father of our Jew, came in and heard my father cursing, he said, "Leave him be, Anton! Why make the child suffer for it?" Then he would call me into the room behind the shop where he always sat and give me a coin, or have something brought for me to eat. I took the coin and ate what I was brought, but I said not a word in thanks. I resented him for my father's sake, though he had done nothing to my father. But I felt he was kind to me to comfort me for my father's cruelty. What was it to him if my father threw pieces of iron at me and cursed me? That was my business and my father's and not the Jew's.

I should have told the Jew: My father has the right to throw stones at me and curse me. I'm not to blame, you say? What do you and I know of it! Why shouldn't I be part to blame for my mother's sin? I wasn't there when she conceived me, you say? But I was meant to be, and that is why she had to conceive me. He loves me, despite how I was conceived, why else would he curse me? Doesn't he curse because he loves me, and throw stones at me because the thought of it still torments his heart fourteen years later? If he didn't love me, he would drive me away. But he wants me to be near him, because he loves me, and I want to be near him and comforted by no one, because I love him, and I want him to be my father and no one else, no matter how it happened, and no matter that I am not called Anton like him, but Alexander.

I said that even as a boy I possessed great physical strength. Let me add, though, that I was of slender build and that my movements were not the least bit awkward, as very strong people's often are. My face was said to be handsome and well-proportioned, and I mention that because it belongs here. I have black hair, my face is narrow and my skin is swarthy like the skin of those who live in southern lands. No one in town had hair as black and glossy as mine, and no one had skin so dark. People smiled and winked at each other when they saw me. But I turned red, and if it was one of the boys who smiled, I lunged at him and thrashed him until he cried for help, even if he was older and bigger than I.

My name was also an excuse to mock me. In our town verses would circulate about someone or another who had provoked ridicule, and as a rule one never knew who had started them. These verses echoed after the victim; he read them on the walls of the houses, on gates and fences. They were simple, clumsy verses, children's rhymes, perhaps indeed made up by children. They were sung with a certain intonation that made them stick in the mind. I remember several such verses. The one about me I first heard from a girl I went to school with. Her blond hair was plaited in a stiff knot that stood out from her head like a stick. She called out the verse to me one time when we were standing in front of the school, waiting for the gate to be opened. The verse hit me like the lash of a whip. I looked at the girl, then I flung myself upon her.

No one hearing the rhyme will understand the effect it had. But perhaps they will grasp it once they realize that these words, which I heard every day now, inexplicably anticipated my fate. Perhaps every person harbors an awareness of his future, dark and unformed, like a heavy weight. And perhaps this verse dismayed me so because it touched this dark premonition in my heart.

I shall set the verse down here, in the uneducated language in which it was sung: Alexander — went on a wander — bought himself some sugar-cander.

I am called Alexander, unlike all the other boys in town, and I am dark and slender and I do not resemble them. And I went on a wander and left my home, perhaps because they laughed and winked at each other when they saw me, or because the verse foretold it. But I should have stayed, just as I stayed with my father even when he cursed me. Surely I would have found happiness there. What do I care for the cities, countries, rivers I have seen? I want to stand once more on our market square, with its cobblestones. I want to see the statue of our patron saints again. I want to know now that I have a wife there and sons, that in itself would be good. On my wanderings, I've bought nothing but sugar candy that melted in the mouth, leaving behind only a sickly sweet taste like the morning after a drinking binge.

MELLON, THE "ACTOR"

Had I been asked as a schoolboy whom I considered the most unusual boy in the class, I might have named the most talented, or perhaps the unruliest, a cynic or a rebel against the school's sacred order. Today I know that talent swiftly grasps how easily it can serve every cause, and often its most telling trait is the ability to conform to the ordinary and find a moral justification for this conformity. Seen from a higher vantage point, the victors in life are generally the vanquished. The deaths of the failures shine at times with the nimbus of victory. Today I know who the most unusual boy in the class was. One of the "fallen," one who cast his life away when it demanded crucial concessions from him.

Two of my schoolmates took their own lives, both shortly after graduation. Neither did it from thwarted love, because of poor examination results, illness or debt, both from the knowledge that under certain circumstances death is preferable to life. The one whose story I shall tell was B. K., the actor. Son of a poor widow who eked out a living for herself and her many children with a small shop. Undernourished, light blond hair, a long, prominent nose on which perched a pince-nez secured by a black cord. His face was wrinkled, aged, his chest narrow, concave. His arms, long and thin, flailed in rhythmless movements. As a little boy B. K. had played a dwarf or an old man in a fairy pageant. A newspaper had included a few lines about him in its discussion of the performance. From first to eighth grade he carried the clipping safely tucked away in his pocket. In the yearbook of our graduating class, the future profession given after his name is the one he never betrayed for a single hour in all those years: the acting profession.

A coincidence, a teacher's joke, the wrong answer to a question may have inspired our nickname for B. K. We called him Mellon, a word we derived from the Greek verb "mellein." It strikes me today that this strange word bears a deep, mystical relation to the life and fate of poor B. K. How meaningfully the word's dictionary meanings echo the life of the little actor! Did the boys have a presentiment of this fate when they gave their classmate the nickname?

Under the word "mello" in the dictionary I find:

"a) to be able to, capable of"

So it began. As a boy he was able to portray an old man, he was capable of it, he was mentioned in the paper, for one day he tasted the vanities of a renown whose memory he still carried in his pocket ten years later. He had no doubt he was able. In my room, at the age of sixteen, wrapped in my cape as if in a prayer shawl, rocking his upper body and gesticulating helplessly with his arms, he performed Shylock for me, his red-rimmed eyes flickering, his pale cheeks flushed with excitement. In school he recited the great classical roles, and how he stood before us, glowing, Egmont, Max, the sorcerer's apprentice, the Good Man, Agamemnon, Achilles, oblivious to the impression made on us by the wobbly pince-nez, the flailing arms, the wretched body in contrast to the lofty words his mouth spoke. No one dared to laugh openly. We know what Mellon was like when offended: a madman who bit and scratched, whose muscleless arms were suddenly filled with toughness and tenacity not easily bested.

"b) to be about to, to intend, to mean to; c) want"

He knew what all this was: being just about to, intending, meaning. It was the "not yet." All was: wanting. And he did not forget about school, as others would have done in his place. For he lived under the sign of his word in all its gravity: "*to mellon*, the future, what is to come." He sat in the first row, attentive and well-prepared. What was all this? Only a being-about-to, let no difficulties arise, that was all, this mountain had to be scaled as quickly as possible.

"d) to hesitate, falter, to be filled with doubts"

No, in truth, he did not hesitate, he did not falter, he had no doubts. What the will of his benefactors set before him, he put behind him, school, what had to be, according to definition e) of his fate. For as yet he "had to" live and prevail in other fields than his own, for the sake of "the future, what is to come."

When he left school, bearing the stamp of his will, God's decree rose up against him in the form of benevolent uncles and protectors of widows. He was to go straight into business, for the protectors of widows and orphans found that what he wanted was wrong and harmful for him. He fell sick. For now he no longer had to. Now there was no more wanting, no being-about-to, no intending, to mellon, the future was no longer: not yet, was now: over. Now he hesitated, his soul faltered and his heart was filled with doubts. “Mello apechesthai Dei, I may, or I must be hateful to Zeus, I am presumably, probably hateful to the deity.” Wasn’t that one example for the usage of the word “mello”? Once more he wanted, because he wanted nothing more. His body was like a child’s body when his soul won its victory over the future that menaced him, and his mouth, which he had believed was made for great and splendid words, closed itself firmly to all nourishment.

And so the poor actor Mellon, nineteen years old, starved himself to death.

BOBEK MARRIES

Fat Uncle Bobek nodded and waved at his guests, he laughed and drank and laid his well-padded hand on the hand of his bride, widowed Mathilde Klosterhoun, who cast down her eyes and smiled. The bride sat next to her daughter Selma. She wore a low-cut sleeveless dress with a rose pinned to it. She smiled when spoken to as deaf people smile, reluctant to admit that they have not understood.

Uncle Bobek ate and talked and laughed. He slurped and smacked his lips, he cracked the bones with his teeth and sucked out the marrow. Uncle Bobek unbuttoned his vest, he drank to Mathilde and his new son-in-law. He set down the beer glass and spread his arms out wide.

"Let's sit together till day breaks, my dear ones, yes indeed! Let's eat and drink and speak with one another! Eat and drink all you can hold, I say, in my honor, in my second wife's honor, and in the honor of Selma's child, my godchild or grandchild, now that she's a grandmother, the young woman. I'd never have thought it either, that it'd turn out this way after all, but you see, I bear no grudges. It's a feeble baby, my godchild, but with God's help it'll live. Why not trust in God's help, I always say. Look at me, I say, I trust in God and I bear no grudges. Doesn't everything appear in a mellow light when we eat and drink?"

First they'd drunk a corn brandy, and then they ate soup

with mushrooms and chicken livers from big, deep soup-plates. Uncle Bobek cut big chunks of bread into it and snapped them up from the spoon. Then the maidservant brought a wooden cutting board with thick-sliced veal and pork and bowls of sauerkraut and dumplings. Between the windows stood a keg of beer. Uncle Bobek had broached the keg himself. Now they ate stuffed chickens. Uncle Bobek chewed up the bones and spat them back onto the plate. At short intervals he drank a schnapps, leaning back with wide-open mouth to toss it down his gullet.

Uncle Bobek ate and drank. He laughed, he waved, he slapped his thighs with his little padded hands. He sighed blissfully when he crushed a choice morsel against his palate. Everything appeared in a mellow light when Uncle Bobek ate and drank. Next to Selma sat the teacher Leopold. He wore a black suit with a white silk handkerchief peeping out of the left breast pocket. In silence Teacher Leopold cut his meat into tiny pieces and chewed the bites tirelessly with his mouth shut tight.

"Eat, eat, Herr Professor," said Uncle Bobek. "You see, you're not keeping pace! Yes, yes, that's what they say these days, chew each bite on both sides of the mouth, don't ask me how often, that's what they say. But where would that get you, I ask. We couldn't eat a third as much, believe you me, Herr Professor, there'd be no time, and you'd be full and tired that much sooner. You have to dig in with a vengeance, I say."

At Uncle Bobek's left sat the flour agent Polatschek. He was short and bald and a friend of Uncle Bobek's youth. Polatschek wore a flower in his buttonhole. He spoke in a high, hoarse voice. From time to time Frau Polatschek, who sat next to her husband, laced up high and dressed in pale-blue silk, laid a hand on Polatschek's arm and whispered warningly: "Polatschek!"

"Just like it was back then," said Uncle Bobek. "Isn't that so, Polatschek?" He dropped a heavy hand onto Polatschek's shoulder. "Look me in the eyes, old friend!"

Polatschek raised his glass.

"Long live the young couple!"

Everyone raised their glasses and drank. Teacher Leopold stood and bowed to Uncle Bobek and Mathilde, holding his glass in front of him.

"And all of you besides!" cried Uncle Bobek. "You're all so good to me, well do I know it. You came, every one of you. You didn't leave me all alone, no, no. It's just like it was back then, when I took my dear departed Martha. There you sit, eating and drinking, let us be content! Back then, when we got married, my dear departed Martha and I, we held the feast at the inn in Pudonitz. How she looked, a virgin, sure as God will stand by me in my final hour, I, Bobek, was the first, and none but me. But today I bear no one any grudges, no no. You're innocent, dear Mathilde. What fault is it of yours? But it can't be brushed aside, the bride's not the one that was, Polatschek! Ah, yes, that was a woman! Sentimental and forever in church. I can see her now, sitting beside me on our wedding day. We're eating at the inn in Pudonitz, the thirty of us, men and womenfolk, and even the oldest don't knuckle under, soup, veal, pork, chickens, two calves and two fat pigs, from head to tail, plus dumplings and sauerkraut by the barrel, and first beer, then schnapps. And not by halves, hahaha! She won't eat, I can't clean my plate fast enough, every mouthful chased by a pint of beer or a tumbler of schnapps. What shouting and singing. You can't hear yourself speak, the way the jaws chomp and the tongues cluck and the lips smack. Martha was nineteen to the day, red spots on her cheeks from the start, doesn't dare to look at me, not a word, sits there staring at the table. When they make jokes about that thingy — you know — the way they always do with newlyweds, she turns red to the roots of her hair, doesn't laugh, not a sound. Sometimes I feel her looking at me sidelong, but when I try to put my hand on her, she shoves me away. The others are already getting up and dancing, the tables are pushed aside. There's a shout from outside, a wagon is there, the lads from Holitz, twelve of them, come to celebrate my wedding. By now I can't stay on my feet. They come, they all sit down at the table, the soup and veal and pork and beer come back out, and I start all over again. Martha says nothing, sits there, the boys drink to her. Toast back, I shout, but she just nods. Then the innkeeper comes up to me, whispers in my ear. What, I say, no kümmel left, no schnapps? The Holitzers are already yelling for schnapps, the meat is fat, they want to drink to the health of the newlyweds, they yell. I'll never live it down, I say to Martha, this disgrace. The innkeeper sends someone around the village, I toast the Holitzers with beer and keep an eye on the door to see if the kümmel has come yet. Someone in the village has got to have kümmel, I think, at the door the innkeeper shrugs his shoulders. Then the Holitzers start to sing. When they're finished I start a new song, to make the time pass, understand? I turn to Martha, 'cause she could have thought of that herself, I think;

and I see, the girl's sitting there, in wedding gown and myrtle, and crying. The tears trickle down into her mouth. Then I felt sorry for her, and 'Don't cry, Martha,' I say, 'the kümmel will come!' And at that the innkeeper actually comes. He got it from a farmer who kept a keg for emergencies. But Martha, God bless her, keeps on crying. She's sentimental. God forgive me, there's no more reason to cry. — But drink, I say, drink, drink, Polatschek! Here we are sitting here, and we're still eating and still drinking. Have we changed, Polatschek? No, no, I say, we're the same as we always were!"

"Polatschek," Frau Polatschek said warningly. "He doesn't tolerate a thing." She turned to Mathilde. "Nothing agrees with him anymore. Food or drink . . . a piece of salami and he's up all night moaning. He ought to do something for his health, I say, and my oldest takes him to task, all right, it costs money, but there are ways! But him? You talk to him!"

Uncle Bobek slammed his fist on the table.

"Go on, go on, wine, I say, bring wine! There's nothing too good or too dear when Bobek celebrates. Look me in the eyes, my dear ones, drink to me and speak with me! We're friends, Uncle Bobek is everyone's friend, Uncle Bobek has no enemies! There are people, you see, that don't understand that, don't drink, they say, it'll be the death of you, and God won't count it in your favor. But I say to you, the wine grows from the earth as does the bread. We'll break the bread together and drink the wine, what does that remind me of? You see, it's taken hold of me! A drinker, a glutton, a belly like a barrel, they say, he'll never get into the Kingdom of Heaven!" He pointed at his plate. "Can that be a sin? The little doves, they fly, the chickens, they peck the grains from the ground. Do you know how many ways there are to cook a chicken? Your Uncle Bobek knows seventeen ways, bitter and sweet and spicy, stuffed and roasted, can that be a sin? Who was that again, what was his name, the one who invented wine?"

"Noah," called Polatschek.

"Noah, there you have it. And who put it into him? God who created everything, you see, from the sun to the kümmel. Where I come from there was one fellow I couldn't keep up with when he sat down and tucked into his food. He closed his eyes at every bite, and we were at the inn one time, and there was hare with sauce and dumplings on the side. But there was something in that sauce that made you whet your tongue on your palate, they were good at that where I come from, and you wrung the juice from the meat between your jaws, down to the last drop, I never ate a hare like that again." The saliva gathered in Uncle Bobek's mouth and ran down his lips. "We didn't want to stop. Then he laid down knife and fork and closed his eyes, and he chewed and smacked his lips, and do you know what he did, my dears? That's the work of God, he said, praised be the name of the Lord! You see, and he wept. One man, he listens, you see, and another man looks, and the third he closes his eyes and tastes. When he was old they told him to hold back, his eyes were weak, otherwise he'd go blind. Do you know what he said to them? I've seen my fill, he said, but I've haven't eaten my fill by far. He was fat and God-fearing all his life. When a man has money, you see, one stows it away in the cupboard, another goes into business, a third swears by wine and good food. Who gives it to the poor? I'm a charitable man for sure. Just tell me a sad story, and it goes straight to my heart and brings the tears to my eyes, no one can come and speak out against me if it should come over me again, today or tomorrow."

Uncle Bobek sank into meditation. Mathilde rose to fetch a cloth. Uncle Bobek had spilled the schnapps over the table.

"That's enough now," said Mathilde.

Uncle Bobek had rested his head on his arms and closed his eyes. His mouth was open, and he breathed deeply. Teacher Leopold was the first to rise and take his leave.

"Herr Bobek is tired," he said, "it's time to go." He kissed Mathilde's hand.

Mathilde did not reply, for at that moment a long drawn-out sound came from Uncle Bobek's mouth, emerging from deep within his body. Uncle Bobek opened his eyes, blinking, and waved a mollifying hand.

"Your forgiveness," he said. "To be human is to be weak. At my age it's hard to hold your own. It was a young wine, dear Mathilde!"

THE SECRET WAR

In the summer evenings the girls stood by the well. Their sleeves were rolled up, they giggled, and when they sauntered off the water sloshed from the jugs and pails. The soldiers stopped and chatted and laughed with them. We were fifteen years old. In front of the soldiers and each other the girls were ashamed of knowing us. When they were alone, after taps or coming and going in the dark alleys, they weren't ashamed.

That began my secret war with R., which no one knew of but the two of us. R. had seen us at the well, there were no two ways about it, but in school he didn't let on. He paced up and down in the classroom as always and drilled us on verbs: "I will have known," "oh, if only I had known," "may we have known," the questions jumped from one boy to the next, as rapid and mechanical as ever. But it could be no coincidence that he stood before me that evening. He must have been at the well unseen and followed me.

It was ten in the evening when red-haired Anna left the well. I approached her as she turned onto a side street. We whispered together for five minutes. Even if he had been standing in the shadow of a house right next to us he wouldn't have been able to hear what we said. Anna went into the house with the pail of water. A moment later she returned. I followed her at a distance. She didn't want to be laughed at for going with me. Girls were still coming down the street from the well. My face was round and still smooth as a child's face. Red-haired Anna was the prettiest girl at the well, big and broad-hipped.

We sat on a bench in the park by the river. That was prohibited at night. But the nearest policeman stood on the road far away, and you could be as undisturbed here as you'd be in the forest. I gave Anna a chocolate bar, a necklace I had won at a shooting gallery, and five crowns, which for a long time she refused to take. She was very good to me. My hands were rough from work, but she let me feel the skin on her neck and chest, how soft and warm it was. Anna had nothing on under the blouse, no corset, only a loose, low-cut shift.

Suddenly we heard soft footsteps, and a dark-lantern flashed. I could see nothing, but I heard a harsh voice. Then Anna began to scream, they had grabbed her, it was two policemen, they dragged her away. A plainclothes officer held me by the jacket. "What did you give her?" he asked. I told him the truth. Then he said something very insulting about my childish appearance. I would rather not repeat it. "Will anything happen to her?" I asked. "See that you get on home," said the plainclothes officer.

Let me say right now that I saw Anna again several months later. She came walking past the well. The girls called her bad names because the police had her in their health book* now. She was prettier than before and dressed like a lady. I don't know why I didn't dare to go up to her.

When the plainclothes officer let go of me I ran away in shame and despair. For a long while I heard Anna's shrieks and screams, like a reproach. When I emerged from the park, R. was standing in front of me in the light of the first lantern. It seemed to me he was smiling.

I ran home. No doubt about it: R. had sent the police. Now would come the aftermath in school. Expulsion from all of Austria's institutions. Manual labor, or a shop apprenticeship, if anyone would still have me. I spent a sleepless night. If I was expelled, I resolved to die. By noon tomorrow it would be decided. But there was no doubt what the decision would be. Toward morning I wrote my parents a farewell letter.

R. said nothing the next day. I spent a second night like the first. Now I understood. There was no doubt in my mind that R. was my enemy, cruel, vengeful, cunning. He was saving the disclosure for later. He would finish me off when the time seemed ripe; until then he would toy with me, swathe me in the illusion of security, humiliate me, torment me. I couldn't bear it. When he asked me: "I will have been eaten," "be an eaten one," I refused to answer. Let it come to a head. Today, right now. My life was done with. But R. held back. No one guessed the secret war between me and R. In the middle of the dictation I laid down my pen: "You're dictating too fast!" — "You're being obstinate," he said, that was all. The next day, leaving the classroom, he said to me: "Your father came to see me." I bolted after him. "You told him, you rat!" I screamed. "You scoundrel!" But my voice had rusted in my throat. Then I fell to the ground.

They carried me into the archaeological cabinet. When I came to, he said: "You'll have to stay home for a few days, you're ill." When vacation began, I heaved a sigh of relief. But it was three more years until graduation. I surrendered. I knew I was hopelessly in his hands. Not until I left school was I released from the burden that jolted me awake at night, was I able to live again.

I met R. in a train compartment many years later. It was after the war. He was traveling to the countryside to buy provisions. His suit was shabby. He recognized me at once. He spoke of my classmates, knew the fate of every one. He spoke guilelessly, as if to a good old acquaintance. I could not shake my sense of diffidence. I feared he could say now what he had not said then, and at that moment I did not realize that I could laugh at it now. But he said nothing today either. "I always thought the world of you," he said. I thought of the awful years. Had he forgotten our secret war? He got off at a small station. From the platform he waved at me one more time. He carried an empty rucksack on his back. There he stood, old and shabby, the burden of my youth! Didn't he remember?

In the end, in the end he never even knew . . .

THE BROTHERS

The brothers met, as agreed by letter, in the express train. At the junction the younger brother joined the older in his compartment. They came from different parts of the world.

They had not seen each other for two years. Now they shook hands without a word, then for a fraction of a second each waited for the other to make the first move toward a brotherly embrace. Nothing happened, and the expectation straining their faces slackened, the smile of reunion fled from their cheeks. They sat across from each other in the empty compartment. The train began to move.

After a few words the conversation flagged. The older brother looked out the window into the night. That's already home, he thought, those woods. Those lights give away a village whose name I once heard in my youth. If that name is spoken, I will remember. In two hours I'll be home. I wanted to embrace my brother. Why didn't I do it?

The younger brother had picked up a newspaper. But he did not read. We're going home together, he thought. In two hours we'll be there. Why are we silent? Do we have nothing to say to each other? I looked forward to this reunion. Why was I ashamed to kiss him? The cold strangeness would have fled, and we would have been close as we were as boys.

They got off the train at midnight at a station where a

carriage was supposed to be waiting. They had another hour's carriage ride ahead of them. The square in front of the little station building was deserted. They decided to wait. The driver must be running late. The cramped waiting room was filled with pipe smoke and the perspiration of sleeping farmers and soldiers. The brothers decided to wait outside the building. They paced side by side, shivering slightly.

The younger brother suggested that they start out on foot and have their baggage picked up from the station the next morning. If the carriage did come, it would pass them on the road. The older brother consented. The silent pacing back and forth with his brother, the inescapable accord of their steps was unbearable.

There seemed to have been a long rain. The road was sodden and filled with puddles. A narrow track on the edge had been trodden dry by pedestrians. They walked in single file. A few minutes later they reached the first village. A dog began to bark, then a second, a third. On the left stood a big building with dimly-lit windows.

Wirnitz mill, both of them thought.

Now, they knew, came the hollow road. It led to the ridge, and their birthplace was on the other side. This far they had come on their walks with their father, and on the way home, when they asked, he had named the constellations by their mysterious names. What an enigmatic world loomed here above the hollow road! Elsewhere the sky was not so full of mysterious horror, nowhere else had they gazed so tremulously at Libra and Cassiopeia.

Would they be stirred again this night as they once were?

On both sides lay the woods where they had played as boys. To the left, the ridge of the Rovna. Would they still tremble when they entered the forest, every moment expecting an animal to leap at them, a wolf, now that they knew there were no wolves in these parts? Off to the left a dog barked again: Oh, that's a dog from Vintavka, they thought. And they smiled with joy at recognizing him after all these years.

The older brother walked behind the younger. The world began beyond the hollow road, he thought. Everything up to the road was home. Oh, why did we leave home? What did we seek that made us go abroad? We had our brother and parents. Where was I sheltered, if not there? I love a woman, but is she not strange, impenetrable, at heart untouched by me? And the man who walks ahead of me, silent, wrapped tightly in his coat, is he not closer and more familiar to me than anyone else in the world? What drove us to part, to leave the place of our birth?

The older brother remembered one time they had driven down the hollow road, in the other direction than today. At that time the younger brother still lived at home. The older brother's throat had tightened with the ache of departure. When they had left the road behind the younger boy said: "You're heading out into the world now."

Hostile feeling flickered behind these words. The older brother realized that the younger would not stay either. Should he have told him that he had found nothing beyond the road but confusion of the heart and the yearning for home? And that he sought nothing now but the way back? But there is no way back, my brother, he should have said then, rather than keeping silent. But the younger boy would have laughed spitefully: He is my enemy, he would have thought.

A carriage rattled down the road toward them. Was it their belated carriage? The younger brother turned around. The moon shone in his face. It was gray and old, but it smiled.

"Our road," he said with a nod.

"Our road," said the older brother, and that was all. He could have added something, a word of love or simply: my brother. But how to overcome his shame?

uncollected stories

SANATORIUM

Hans Suchander is lying in a white room, all white. Tall green trees rustle their fragrance into the room. This air is good for sick lungs, say the doctors.

Suchander lies in his room all day long, staring at the ceiling. From time to time he coughs.

Suchander's hands are constantly cold and damp, like his brow. But he is not in any pain. He feels a pleasant slackness in his joints, a voluptuous lassitude in his feet.

Sometimes he thinks: "If only one didn't have to die! So young!"

But he is too tired to think about it for long or struggle with death. He's so weak, after all, so tired!

When the nurse comes, he smiles.

On sunny days they roll Hans Suchander into the garden in a wheelchair. They also wheel out the pale girl with the horrible cough.

Suchander and Lo sit across from each other, seldom speaking. By turns Lo and Suchander reach for the little green bottle with the metal cap which both keep next to them.

She's so pale and so thin, thinks Suchander. Poor Lo. How young she is! And what a horrible cough she has. She won't live long either. Lo is going to die soon, even sooner than I.

"Are you feeling better today?" Lo asks. Suchander gives a faint nod.

Poor boy, she thinks. Soon he must die. He's past helping, the nurse said. What a horrible cough he has! And what hectic spots on his cheeks.

"I hear you're a student. What do you study?"

"I wanted to become a musician."

"You must play something for me."

"The doctor has forbidden it. It agitates me . . . I haven't played for a long time."

Lo drowses. Her frail chest rises and falls fitfully. Lo smiles.

A miracle could save me, me and Lo, thinks Suchander. A miracle. He shuts his eyes.

For us, he thinks, there's no more spring, no summer. No seasons at all. No love, no friendship. We just lie calmly and wait. Wait for death. Maybe we should pray that we won't die yet. That we'll go on living; just go on living somehow, chained sick to our beds if need be. How long is it since I was young? I walked, I talked with many people, I made music. How long is it since I was a child? I went to school with a satchel. I was the only one in the class who had a brown satchel with nickel buckles. Even then I was always quieter than the other boys. I didn't want to play with them. Maybe it was because death was in me even then, when I was very young. I feel as if I'm old now, very old. Sometimes I feel as if the nurse is impatient with me already, as if it's taking too long.

"When am I going to die, Nurse?" Suchander asks softly so as not to wake Lo.

The nurse looks up from her book.

"Oh, this time next year you'll be up and about again."

The nurse has watched many people die. She has said this to many people.

Suchander smiles. Maybe it's possible after all, he thinks. Maybe. —

They've stopped wheeling Lo into the garden. The loneliness weighs so heavily on Suchander that he prefers to stay in his room as well.

"Why doesn't Lo come out into the garden anymore?" he asks the nurse over and over again.

"Lo is very sick," says the nurse.

"Then I want to see her!"

"The doctor has forbidden it, you heard him!"

"Will she come back soon? Or will it be much longer?"

"I think! . . . I don't know."

And Suchander knows that pale Lo has stopped coughing, that she was carried out at night as so many have been carried from this house, secretly, in the dark, as he, too, will probably be carried soon. He asks no more: he doesn't want to hear it, hear that Lo is now dead.

Did Lo struggle hard with death, or did she fall asleep, never to wake again? It must be terrible to drift off unsuspecting! Away from the sun, light, from girls, men, children, away into a tremendous abyss! Even if you can't see them, it's wonderful to know of all the things, trees, dogs, circuses, cafés, music, snow, dances — how many things there are! — to know of everything, everything! And then . . . Nothing! Forgotten! Nothing means: infinite empty black horror. They ought to find a cure for death. Nothing is impossible! The doctors, all humanity ought to do nothing else, day and night: only search tirelessly for a cure . . . Too late! Suchander is lost. Hopelessly. This body, yes, this damp weak body, this hand resting on the blanket, his hand, doomed to decompose . . . to perish!

Suchander sits up with an effort.

"Nurse," he says, "Nurse, you must help me!"

The nurse looks at him uncomprehendingly, feelingly.

"I must have had a bad dream, that's all," he says.

Suchander sinks back into the cushions. With a fine cloth the nurse dries the sweat from his brow.

LETTER TO A WOMAN

Madam!

Yesterday, when I was drifting aimlessly through the crowded streets again as I so enjoy doing, I suddenly saw you before me. For the space of a moment your gaze rested upon me, surprised at the sight of me; then you had passed me by. I turned around. You took your companion's arm. For a few seconds more I could make out your brisk little feet, then all had vanished.

Madam, how long has it been? It was before the war. I remember it as vividly as if it were yesterday, how we parted on the railway platform in Vienna, how I was left behind gazing after the waving white handkerchief as the train slowly left the station hall and took you with it. I remember these five autumn days as vividly as if six years hadn't passed since then. Five autumn days, five happy autumn days! Striking up an acquaintance in the overcrowded train en route from a summer resort by a lake in the mountains, and then five days stolen from reality, five hidden days, secret days, irretrievably vanished days! An episode? Don't say that. An episode is something to smile at. But I don't think you will smile at those days either. You too, Madam, must have felt yesterday on the arm of your companion, your husband perhaps, that what binds us together is not a faded memory, but still-living happiness within us.

Do you remember the trip to Rodaun? Do you remember the out-of-the-way picture gallery where a decrepit attendant foisted naïve explanations of the paintings upon us? (What did we care about the paintings!) How the tip failed in its objective and only made the old man feel obliged to give us a real tour of the halls? Do you remember how we had supper together in the garden of the restaurant? It was so chilly that we had to huddle together. And do you remember the homely student's lodgings in the 9th District? You came for five minutes, you came just to have a look at it, on the last, the very last of these happy days, and you stayed for two hours, making us late for the opera, they were playing "Traviata," yes, "Traviata," I remember it so well!

Before your train left, I said: This cannot be a parting for good. Fate can't wish us to be happy for a mere five days. But you were the better prophet. You didn't believe this happiness could be resumed again one day. Perhaps that wasn't what you wanted, either. And perhaps you were right. Perhaps the greatest happiness is the one which passes quickly, like our five days, leaving not even a little tag-end to hold the happiness by, a shabby little corner, no, one which is suddenly gone once and for all. You didn't even leave me your address! I knew only that you were going to a man you also loved. And that was no contradiction for me. It was all so wonderful.

Now I see you again, wrapped in a fur which just barely reveals your eyes and a bit of your nose. In the crowd of strangers we pass at a distance and no one suspects how very close we were for a little space of time. Six years ago in the fall, when we were six years younger . . . We let everything sink away around us, we were on a desert island five days long, nothing on all sides but our happiness. Oh, how foolish we were, how foolish I was to forget to begin preparing a reunion even then! Or was it wise not to think of it in those few hours, not to torment you, not to press you, not to beg you to contrive ruses under whose cover we could have hastened back to each other? Was it wise to think of nothing in those days but that happiness, that embrace, that kiss, that kiss always given and enjoyed afresh and always for the last time? I am as foolish now as I was then, Madam, and since that time I have often fallen very foolishly in love with women. You see, I have the great good fortune not to understand women. And thus I am still able to thrill as I did then to a little movement of the hand, to a laugh which those unfortunates who imagine they understand women might call coquettish, and gratefully kiss a hand and believe it for an hour when a woman says she loves me. The love of a woman still stirs me and brings me to surrender. And though I have since experienced many an hour which I would not care to see stricken from my life, the happiness of our five fall days still shines upon me more blissfully than any other light. Those were days which fell between the wheels of time, which we saved, knowing that in this moment we had to consummate them for all time at every step, knowing that even as we enjoyed them, we lost them.

When I held you in my arms, slender, browned by the summer sun, you asked: "Do we know if it's a deep feeling or just a whim?" I believe I replied: "Do we ever know? And is that the most important question? See, aren't these days like a dream?"

— You: “If it was a whim, it’s good that it will soon be over. If it was a deep feeling, we will think of these days and be glad. And maybe we will see each other again.” — Of course there’s no logic in that. But twilight was in the room, you were so beautiful and you said it so beautifully and you snuggled up to me. I could have cried, I was so happy.

Now I have seen you again. You passed me and your eyes rested on me for one moment. After that I wandered the streets for a long time. Then I went home and wrote this letter. Perhaps this newspaper will fall into your hands. Perhaps you will read this letter which is meant for you. I do not want to play fate and resume what is over. I only want you to take a visiting card — do you still have those long, slim cards with a reddish sheen? — take a card and write me (no more than that): “I remember it fondly too!”

I kiss your hands in deep gratitude . . .

A DREAM

. . . . . . took form from leaves and trees, raised his sword above his head, swung it at me menacingly. Several times he whirled the tree around his head like that, high in the air, the branches whistling. I thought I'd go deaf from that stupendous whistling. He came at me like that and I recognized him when I saw his head which he held in his hand and threatened to throw at me. I couldn't escape and I couldn't cry out and I was terribly afraid of that bloody mass of raw meat, the kind that hangs on the butcher's racks, afraid it would hit me cold and wet in the face. I screamed until all the castle's halls slipped past me down to the very last one, where Mother stood. She bent down to the ground and said she'd lost the footman because a fire had broken out. And my aunt burst out of the hut with Marie and they had the big black pans of cherry strudel in their hands and they screamed and ran off down the street. So I went back to playing Indians with my brother Felix and suddenly I saw that he was bleeding from the chest, a triangular scrap of skin had come off, I thought of Christ and was still crying when the professors sat down at the table to test me. The one with the long beard asked me for the indicative of Herod, which I recited in flawless Russian. The man with the long beard didn't recognize me, but I saw the bloody triangle gleam under his beard. I didn't know why my brother was speaking Russian with me, like on the ship at Sevastopol in the sailors' mutiny.* I'd cut up the meat and the sailors came in and laughed and ate it raw. I shuddered because I had the cat's pelt around my chest where my mother had tied it so I wouldn't catch cold on my way to school through the snow. Then I reached the statue of Cyril and Methodius at the crossroads and wanted to go into the brickworks before the dogs began to bark, it was frightful how they barked, especially the butcher's. It surprised me that they didn't start barking and that all the girls from town were going to the well with prayer books and the bells began to ring, even though it was Easter, only our maid was away and not back by ten in the evening and Grandmother was afraid because it was evening and people are superstitious, afraid of wild dogs, you hear them all over town and when you're on the road you hear them from the villages all around. I had to hurry to reach the village where Father had gone, and they'd brought the bicycle he rode and it was bloody and the people said: Yes, at the inn in Lysice. But the Members of Parliament were waiting for me and sent me to the chancellery for the authorization and Teacher Mayer cursed me out for my fingernails before giving me the authorization. I read it: MP Pernerstorfer. And I cried bitterly because I was shot dead and asked my brother to help me up, but he only raised his hand so I'd hear and now I heard it too. It was a tremendous din, the same din from the very start, a din of bells, I'd heard it from the very start, always in my ears, all the bells from the villages, they all rang out at once and I couldn't tell which ones they were. But I tried very hard. On the balcony Felix pointed down at the street, the lads whistled, wanted us to come down, the doors were locked, on a rope or the drainpipe. But the bells rang so loud we couldn't. So I kept going and entered the woods, the copse, the copse started beyond the bastion and I found Svetly from third grade again with his face gone blue hanging on a little sapling. I remembered it vividly from earlier, I remembered that I'd known it the whole time and I'd talked about it with everyone. And I was very scared and wanted to get out of the woods. The girls whispered at the front doors and in the dark corners and I wanted to turn to them, and I heard someone calling from the kitchen, because the door was open and they were baking for the holidays, but I couldn't go any further and had to sit down, right next to the mill where our Loisie was looking out the window, but she just scolded me because I was sitting in the middle of the tracks and the train was coming, the midday train that didn't stop and there was no one nearby and the people screamed and waved flags but no one could help, I was tied to the tree and wanted to scream but I couldn't and I cried because I had such awful worries. So Grandmother baked me an apple and I was about to eat it when I remembered that Grandmother was dead, when Father cried so much and Uncle Max, I never would have thought it and I refused to believe it. Grandmother scared me, but then I laughed because she was probably just doing it because I had the hiccups, to make it go away by scaring me, and that was why all the bells were ringing. But now the shooting had started. I ran back down the road until I came to Red Pond and was told that the Battle of Königgrätz was about to start here, and I was scared because I'd learned this battle and couldn't help. I was about to dismount from my horse when they came from all sides, all yellow, the Russians out of the ground, and I turned around because I was supposed to help pull the fire engine out of the fire station, because they'd seen the awful glow of fire in the black sky from our window off toward Sebranice. People ran past the house and the dogs barked and my sister cried when father ran out onto the street. But the policeman Vavra noticed and he took away our marbles and thrashed us one by one and I wanted to hurry and recite the Battle of Königgrätz anyway before it was all over, but the sergeant-major waved me away because the regional school inspector had already gone into the room some time ago. He ate with Father and wine and roast pork were served and they ate it together and I stood outside the brickworks and I remembered everything and I was sad and it was very dark and I had to cry very hard . . .

BIBA IS DYING

The attendant found Doctor Schneeberger, First Assistant at the pediatric clinic, making his rounds in the ward.

"Telephone — Herr Doctor is asked to come home immediately."

"What's the matter?"

"I was told Herr Doctor is asked to come. Directly."

"Colleague," he said to one of the other young doctors, "I don't know what the matter is — at any rate, please finish making the rounds!"

In front of the clinic he waved down a passing cab, gave his address and got in. No doubt some unnecessary foolishness on the part of the governess. What could possibly have happened? He'd ask the cab to wait and go straight back. At eleven he had his course to give. He was going to present little Willy. Very interesting lymphogranulomatosis. A classic case with all the symptoms. He smiled with satisfaction at the thought of the little boy. So rare to find the real thing. Always little deviations, despite the city's wealth of material. Like so many things you simply have to believe, time and time again, without seeing them in nature for yourself. Not in perfect condition, anyway. But this Willy was a joy. And there was no time to lose. No telling how much longer one would have this case at one's disposal. He was failing visibly, judging by all the indications.

He hurried up the stairs to his apartment. The governess opened the door. Her eyes were red, and she did not even give him time to take off his coat.

"Thank God," she said, sobbing. "Thank God! I'm at my wit's end."

"What's . . ."

She pointed to the nursery door.

"What, what is it?" he cried. Without waiting for a reply, he opened the door.

"Biba, Biba," he said, going up to the bed where the two-year-old lay.

Biba's eyes were open. He looked at his father, but without smiling as usual. His face was red with heat. He breathed heavily.

Washing his hands, Doctor Schneeberger asked:

"The night passed calmly?"

"He slept soundly, Herr Doctor. He woke at seven as usual. I didn't notice a thing."

She dried her tears with a crumpled handkerchief.

"Where were you yesterday?"

"Out walking from eleven to one, as usual. Everything as always, as Herr Doctor ordered. I follow . . ."

"Bowel movement?"

"Not yet today. But twice yesterday."

"Yes," said Doctor Schneeberger, as if there were a question he had to answer.

Then he bent over the child. He drew back the blanket, raised the nightshirt. The firm little body glowed against his ear. The child's head lay tilted back, motionless. The doctor reached quickly to take his pulse.

He rose. He covered the child up again. The governess looked at him. He buttoned up his jacket.

She's not the mother, he thought. She won't make a scene.

"We've come too late," he said. The governess recoiled. Doctor Schneeberger grasped her hand. "Hush," he said forcefully, "Hush."

"Herr Doctor, help, that can't . . . our Biba, our Biba . . ."

Our Biba, our . . . My Biba, oh God, my Biba! What did she want, why didn't she leave him alone. He wanted to tell her that he wished to be alone with his son. But he could not utter a word. The governess understood him. She fell silent. She turned slowly and went.

If he had a mother, thought Doctor Schneeberger, it wouldn't have come to this. A mother would have sensed it this morning, yesterday. He sat on the bed.

"Biba, Biba," he said.

The boy stared straight ahead.

No reaction to auditory stimulation, something inside Doctor Schneeberger thought. One could see whether . . .

He did not finish the thought. His throat contracted. He flung himself upon the boy, pressed the hot head against his cheek.

"Biba, Biba," he sobbed, "do you recognize me, your father? I love you, Biba. You're all I have. Don't go, don't go! I've seen so little of you, Biba, my duties . . . No, no . . . that was bad of me, you have no mother. Quite right, Biba, you don't recognize me . . . !"

He got to his feet. Rescue the child, rescue him! A clear-cut, obvious case. There's no help for it. Still, a miracle, just this once a miracle! . . . Why aren't there any miracles?

He drew a chair up to the bed and sat on it.

"Biba," he said, "it's a matter of hours!" Is the governess standing behind the door? "Your father knows it for certain. Meningitis epidemica. Classic case. My little Biba, moribundus, that's his name, my one and only beloved Moribundus, your father is speaking to you. Your father knows everything, where the rigor mortis starts, when the limbs stop responding to stimuli, he knows it with the one brain which is a doctor's brain, a good doctor's brain, maybe one of the best in the city, and with the other brain he refuses to know it, refuses to take note of the symptoms he sees, which his experience confirms. All he wants is to be your father, Biba, Biba, he wants you to hear him, even though it's impossible, wants you to reach out your arms and say one more time in your voice: Biba loves Papa. Say it, Biba, say it one more time!"

Biba tried to sit up. He looked at his father. Schneeberger had gotten to his feet. The look Biba gave him was imploring, reproachful. You're letting me die? said the look.

Doctor Schneeberger spread his arms:

"I can't . . . Bernhard." He realized that he couldn't call him Biba now, the boy whose last gaze he met, that the dying boy was no longer Biba, barely his son now, an old man, with no sweet nickname.

Biba closed his eyes.

"Exit," Doctor Schneeberger said tonelessly. "Exit, exit!" he shouted, the word maddened him, but he could not think of a different, warm word for what was happening, only the cold, worn-out, impartial term of the expert, he shouted it at the walls while tears ran down his face.

The governess stood next to him.

"Biba is dying," said Doctor Schneeberger. And after a pause, as the governess turned away and buried her face in her hands, he added: "Our Biba."

LITTLE LIES

Dialogue for a Married Couple

HE, SHE. — He is sitting at his desk. — She enters. Flushed from her outing. Exaggeratedly animated.

SHE: You're home? I thought you were at the club today. — Hello! — Too bad you didn't tell me. I could have used the car. How long have you been here?

HE: An hour, darling.

SHE: You poor thing! An hour. Oh Lord, they didn't give you your tea. But I walked. I couldn't possibly know you were home already.

HE: You walked?

SHE: Yes. Such splendid weather, after all. I was window-shopping. Wonderful new things everywhere. They're showing the winter fashions already. You must come with me tomorrow, promise?

HE (gives her a long look).

SHE (adjusts her hat, takes her mirror out of her purse): Why are you looking at me like that? What's the matter? Get on with you, you're an odd one! Are you angry because I wasn't home, you . . . (she bends over him. He politely fends her off.) Please! Don't put yourself out! Did the gentleman get up on the wrong side of bed this morning? Good Lord, I couldn't have known you weren't going to the club today after the office, but as you please! I certainly won't molest you with displays of affection.

HE: I don't understand why you're getting so excited. Strange . . .

SHE: Me . . . me excited . . . hahaha . . . You're excited, my boy, because I'm not sitting there waiting for my lord and master to come home. The good wifey! God, what kind of a life am I leading! Sitting at home and waiting, waiting, waiting! — Excited, that's a good one, why should I be excited . . . The idea . . . There's nothing strange, my dear. I'd appreciate your telling me what you find so strange.

HE: Mainly — as I said — the fact that you're so excited, darling.

SHE: Mainly! And then . . . There's more to come, if I follow you.

HE: Well, a trifle. An optical peculiarity, if you will.

SHE: Optical? Now I really don't understand a thing! You're ill, very ill! (She takes a seat.) I'm seriously concerned. But explain, what sort of optical peculiarity . . . hahaha.

HE: Gladly. You did say: "I walked," didn't you? But it seems to me I looked out the window and saw you getting out of a . . .

SHE: Oh, it seems that way, does it? Wonderful. So I'm supposed to walk all this way on foot? In this weather! The lord and master takes his 80-hp car, and I'm supposed to walk myself into the ground.

HE: Did I ever ask you to, darling?

SHE: It would be a matter of the utmost indifference to me

if you did ask me to, my friend. I took a taxi, from Uhlandstrasse, it cost two marks sixty to get here, if you want to know the details.

HE: How do you know that?

SHE: Now how might she know that, the little woman? Just think, think hard for a moment, how! I'll divulge the secret. When I got out, I paid. I gave the driver five marks, and he gave me two marks forty in change. I gave him a twenty-pfennig tip. Are you satisfied?

HE: Odd! How my eyes deceived me! I saw you close the door of the taxi and make straight for the house.

SHE: What perspicacity! I paid through the partition, my love. I don't like waiting around on the street.

HE: Oh, pardon me! The possibility didn't occur to me, really it didn't! But these drivers are too stupid for words. No wonder they never get ahead in life.

SHE: The drivers?

HE: Why didn't he switch the taximeter back to "free"? He drove on without switching it back. I saw it perfectly. For "free" the two little lamps to the left and right of the driver light up. The taxi turned at the next corner and drove past me again on the other side of the street, so I got another look at it.

SHE: An interrogation! . . . This is going too far! I simply won't put up with it. Do you understand? I demand to be believed!

HE: What, that you walked home?

SHE: No irony, please! I don't know which of us has more reason to get ironical! At any rate, I won't let myself be interrogated, (with the profoundest scorn in her voice) detective!

HE: I have no intention of interrogating you, darling. But does it take special detective skills to gather that you weren't alone in the taxi?

SHE: Splendid! I wasn't alone in the taxi! Of course I wasn't. I don't see why I should make a secret of that.

HE: Neither do I, my darling. That's just what I don't understand.

SHE: I met Edwin on my way, he asked if he could take me home. I don't understand you, really I don't . . . You never used to be this way. (She raises the handkerchief to her eyes.) Can there be anything more harmless than letting someone take you home when you meet an acquaintance, a friend? Can there be any reason to make a secret of that?

HE: Certainly not, if it was Edwin.

SHE: I won't stand for any doubts.

HE: Why not? Because you told the truth in the first place?

SHE: You're an odd one. You can tell I'm not lying any more. Can't you . . . ?

HE: Don't worry, I couldn't see inside the car. The most I could do now is give Edwin a call . . .

SHE: You won't do that (gets to her feet). I forbid you.

HE: Why do you forbid me?

SHE: . . . I want to keep you from making a fool of yourself. There's nothing more foolish than jealousy.

HE: You don't need to worry about that. It's already superfluous to talk to Edwin.

SHE: That's very intelligent. I knew it . . . really, I know you're intelligent, much, much more intelligent than I am, but you know, I enjoy testing your intelligence, with harmless little lies. But you always see right through them. I'm so proud of you! Say, do you know what the fashionable color is going to be, the absolute fashionable color: blue! What do you say to that?

THE CALIPH

I have no confidante but this paper. That is the wonderful thing about my secret, that I have it all to myself. I smile sometimes to recall that I have excluded all others from my secret. At times I think it would be good to have an initiate. Just one, by no means more. In company we could smile at each other knowingly, and this smile would exclude all others. I would wink at the initiate when I passed him on the street, and alone in a room together we would slap our knees and laugh out loud at the world's stupidity. But whom should I confide in? One, I fear, would not appreciate the secret, another would inwardly mock me, a third would break his secrecy. I am raising myself a trustworthy initiate. It is my son. When he is twenty, perhaps even eighteen, I will let him in on my secret. I will open the cabinet; I will hand him the proof. I have proof, I am not indulging in empty prattle or in innuendoes. My proofs are numbered, dated, the most important under seal. I have saved them, not only to shield myself from doubt and disbelief — what do private concerns matter in the greater scheme of things — but because I feel duty bound before the conscience of the world to save these important documents for future generations.

I must note that I am thought to be nothing but a small-time tradesman. I conduct my business like any other tradesman, visiting my clients and selling confectionery. My clients are the proprietors of small shops in town. I talk to them about the prospects for the harvest, the rising prices, the slow business. I ask about their sons and daughters, about the rheumatism of one, the stomach spasms of the other. I have known my clients for many years. My conversations differ in no way from the conversations of other tradesmen. The difference between me and other tradesmen is my secret. When I display my samples, push the sale, record the order, when I leave the shop with or without success, I am at all times conscious of my secret. I know that no business fiasco can embitter me, any more than the delight at a done deal can be mentioned in the same breath as the other, greater, purer delight in my secret.

I long for the moment when my son will reach adulthood. Discussions of rising prices or politics in his, the initiate's, presence will have the exquisite charm of a comedy which only the two of us understand and which we play out of waggishness when I earnestly expound the views of the tradesman I seem to be. My son will know that I am something quite different and that from whimsy and delight in secrecy I indulge in the little joke of taking seriously the role that others assign to me. He will have inspected the dossiers which reveal to him what I in all secrecy have done.

He will know that his father is a great statesman. A great statesman, yet modest enough to go on playing the small-time tradesman, pursuing without superiority the wretched living of an agent, joining without pride in the naïve conversations of friends and relatives. He'd have good cause to be as proud as the others, my son will think. What have they accomplished and what has he? Through a wise alliance with Russia which I, his son, found in his desk, did he not make that ill-starred year 1866 a peaceful, happy one? Did he not, he whom they take for an insignificant little man, reconcile France and Prussia without a war, through foresighted statesmanship, thus sparing hundreds of thousands in 1870* from death, mutilation and tears? All this, perhaps, because he was free from personal ambition, because his great influence behind the scenes did not tempt him to aspire to the outward brilliance of other statesmen.

So my son may say. I do not know whether he would be saying too much. I am happy to leave that verdict to the future generations who will study the dossiers. I shall say only that my aspiration as a statesman was to secure peace and progress for all the world's peoples. Fate graciously allowed me to prevent all the wars waged by other statesmen of my age. I had the good fortune not to depend on the reports of the diplomats. I had the good fortune to make my decisions in the quiet of my study, without thirsting for the triumph and acclaim of the day, for the ovations of the misguided masses, fully conscious of the grave responsibility God had placed upon me. I weighed the intellectual and economic currents and forces, and I decided impartially, for I never lost sight of the fact that each one of my decisions will reverberate for decades, for centuries, that the face of the world changed the moment the decision left my head and became reality on paper, in notes, letters, treaties and alliances. This is part of my secret's great burden, that the others I speak with do not suspect that I made history take a different path than they imagine. How I smile when I hear and read of the ventures of other statesmen who have choked the world with war and famine. And how my heart lifts at the thought that it was given to me to keep peace and order through — is it presumptuous of me to say so? — the wise exploitation of political opportunities.

I pity the statesmen and those who take their ventures for reality, I pity them and smile. For I know that their deeds are not real; if they were, how could we bear all the pain this statesmanship has brought upon us? I know: all that is real is what I have thought, as recorded in the documents in my cabinet. I know it, and I walk the streets of the city, ride on the roofs of the omnibuses, descend into the shafts of the metro with my secret like Harun al-Rashid. I walk through Baghdad, incognito as the caliph.

In seeking a metaphor for Ungar's artistry, Thomas Mann turns to his "wine-traveler," an "artist in a different sphere" who equates art and intoxication:

> I was surrounded by rich young men and beautiful women I drew after me into the beatitude of pleasure. They had never drunk like this before. I revealed to them the mystery of the wine we drank. In old wine is the scent of all flowers, the rays of the sun, children's laughter, men's sweat, the vision of the summer landscape, all ripe and heavy as the breast of a nursing mother. I did not reveal it in words, my senses revealed it, as women's mute sensuality reveals itself and plunges into sweet transport.

Mann's selection of this passage is both insightful and slightly misleading, pointing to an interesting tension in Ungar and his writing. Ungar's friends knew him as a bon vivant, charming and charismatic; like his wine-traveler, he had a gift for the voluptuous intoxication evoked above. In actual fact, however, he indulged it more often in life than in art. Indeed, in his review of *The Maimed* Berthold Viertel spoke of a language "so sober" that "one does not know whether it is from fever or from frozenness."

Another word used by Ungar's critics was "nakedness." Reviewing *Boys & Murderers*, Stefan Zweig spoke of an "utterly sharp, utterly clear, almost violently naked language," while Viertel spoke of *The Maimed* as having "its very own kind of nakedness, one far less bearable than the nakedness of skin-clothed creatures; it is akin to the nakedness which George Grosz makes phosphoresce under the clothes in his new portfolio 'Ecce homo.'" An apt metaphor: language stripped down so far that it shades into an almost hallucinatory luminescence, the dark side of the lyricism praised by Thomas Mann.

Dieter Sudhoff argues convincingly in his study *Hermann Ungar: Leben-Werk-Wirkung* [Hermann Ungar: Life-Work-Influence] that Ungar's "laconicism" was both a conscious artistic choice and a symptom of the "linguistic isolation" and resultant "linguistic impoverishment" of the German-speaking community in Prague and other parts of Czechoslovakia. While some Prague German writers such as Leppin, Werfel, Rilke and Meyrink sought enrichment in ornamentation and baroque flights of linguistic fancy, others, such as Kafka and Ungar, were "purists," "embracing the limited linguistic material of their environment and making a virtue out of necessity, making it their special ambition to [...] restore to the individual word its original intensity." Sudhoff goes on to suggest that "for both [Kafka and Ungar] contributing factors may have been that they had experience with German legalese; that, as Jews, they felt like mere guests in the German language; and that they combined an idolatry of truth with a skepticism toward language."

As Sudhoff notes, Ungar works with a relatively restricted vocabulary and, on the whole, simple, clear, often rather abrupt sentence structures. He makes sparing use of adjectives and metaphors. And despite his strong connection to his own Jewish heritage and to the surrounding Czech culture, he uses virtually no Czech or Jewish expressions.

The only identifiably Yiddish expression appears in "A Man and a Maid": *Kalle*, the German spelling of "kalleh," meaning more or less "slut." Significantly, the story hinges on this word — it reverberates, as potent and incomprehensible as the sexual urges which it wakens.

The selective use of this Yiddish word allows it to truly regain its "original intensity" (in Hebrew"kalleh" means "bride"). This pivotal word posed a translation problem. Certain Yiddishisms have gained common currency both in German and in English — but not necessarily the same ones, or with the same connotations. "Kalleh" does appear to have the same connotations ("slut" and "bride") in English-Yiddish usage, but it has not entered into the English mainstream. Would "kalleh" have been a recognizable pejorative term for Ungar's contemporary German readers? In that case, I might choose to render it with a common pejorative term such as "slut" or "broad." On the other hand, if "kalleh" was as exotic a word for German readers in the 1920s as for English-speaking readers at the turn of the millennium, it would be more appropriate to leave it as is, merely using the English transliteration. Though unable to settle the question to my satisfaction, I chose the second approach, retaining the strangeness of the word which so perturbs the narrator, and highlighting Ungar's rare use of dialect.

In other ways, too, Ungar's art relies on the skillful placement of emphasis, using single words or indeed bodily utterances (what the critic Anton Kuh called the "bombshell" of "Colbert's Journey") to dramatic effect. He uses rhythm to create tension and express emotion without resorting to ornamental, descriptive language. German is more amenable than English to shifts in word order and sentence structure and to the use of clipped sentence fragments, which Ungar often uses to create momentum, shift tempos and draw attention to key words. I have tried to retain Ungar's rhythm even at the cost of the occasional awkward moments — some of which appear to be a conscious part of Ungar's narrative strategy.

Ungar's eschewal of description, his mastery of rhythm and dramatic emphasis may reflect his theatrical experience. The effect of his first-person stories is that of living monologue, a voice now calmly reporting, now shaking with the effort of self-control, now emotionally numb, now stumbling or finding new fluency in moments of drama. Ungar's narrators tend to be uneducated men who have an obsessive need to tell their story of guilt or trauma, but doubt their own ability to tell it properly. Their shifts in tone, the occasional stiltedness, their "digressions" (put down to "inexperience in storytelling"), their feelings of inadequacy in "explaining" or "describing" are expertly orchestrated and profoundly revealing.

Ungar felt conflicted about his own predilection for the first-person form. The writer Ludwig Winder recalled: "Once, shortly after the publication of the novella collection *Boys & Murderers*, Ungar came to me in a despairing mood and complained that he was unable to get away from the first-person form; he was working on a novel which he wanted to write as an objective account that had nothing to do with the author, but the work stalled when he gave up the first-person form. [...] I tried to console Ungar by pointing out all of the first-person narratives in world literature; I advised him to stick with the first-person form if that was what came naturally to him. 'That's impossible,' he insisted, 'I can't take the risk of having people think that I'm always writing about myself; the thought so paralyzes me that I just can't go on working.'"

In a letter to Thomas Mann, thanking him for his effusive review of *Boys & Murderers*, Ungar wrote: "I doubt whether I have yet mastered the form of the 'third-person narration,' which you also seem to prefer to the 'first-person narration.' It seems to me that in it, the third-person narration, these things you speak of are lost. That is why my novel [*The Maimed*], begun in the first person, is not yet finished, because I am rewriting it in the third person and that naturally requires a different approach. It seems to me that something is lost this way, a certain melancholy which would have suffused the whole, and last but not least the cautiousness of the message, its ultimate indefinability. (All of which, of course, is due only to my lack of technical ability.)" (A version of the first chapter of *The Maimed* in the first person was published in Otto Pick's 1922 anthology *Deutsche Erzähler aus der Tschechoslowakei.* As it contains little new material, we chose not to include it here.)

Certainly Ungar did master the third-person form, but it is unfortunate that notions of its superiority (or perhaps rather the safer distance it offered) should have made him doubt the first-person voice he favored. It is the clearest expression of the humanity overlooked by contemporary critics who regarded his work as depraved, immoral and voyeuristic. The morality of his work lies in the peculiar dignity of his narrators, however monstrous, and the validity of their experience. This is a morality which mistrusts "objectivity" and "messages." Ungar's characters are captives in their own solitary realities, but when they speak for themselves, we realize how ill-equipped we are to judge them from outside. They know themselves, however imperfectly, and they condemn themselves more severely than any outsider could. Even the self-delusion of the "secret caliphs" commands a peculiar respect.

In *The Maimed*, Karl Fanta, the friend of the protagonist, Franz Polzer, has succumbed to a disease which disfigures both his body and his soul. His wife Dora tells Franz:

> "He no longer has a heart. The boils have devoured it too. That's why he is so cruel to me."
> She looked at him steadily. He felt that this explanation of all her suffering was a sort of mystery for her, something she had thought hard about, that one must not contradict.

However strange the stories people tell themselves, Ungar suggests, however bizarre their attempts to make sense of their lives, they are inviolable; it is not for us to contradict them. An insight both sobering and extraordinarily sensitive, it is a luminous moment in a scene of Groszian grotesqueness.

Another instance of this peculiar sensitivity occurs in "Story of a Murder," in the "stranger's" letter to the narrator:

> *I hear that you wanted to become a soldier and have not yet abandoned the thought. I hope that your wishes will be fulfilled, little soldier.* Here something was crossed out. I could not decipher it. Then the text went on: *But if you do not succeed, learn to understand that the time of hope is richer than the time of fulfillment.*

Why does Ungar mention these crossed-out words? We cannot guess what the stranger meant to say — but the effect is of unspoken reservations.

Ungar's own attitude toward the military was conflicted. In the letter to Thomas Mann cited above he wrote: "Doesn't the desire to obey exist alongside the urge toward absolute 'liberté'? I was a soldier, and back then — on the front — I sighed less over my own lot than that of all the others. Back then I was an anti-militarist, a revolutionary; I am finished with politics, but I can relate to soldiership (not to militarism) . . ." In "Story of a Murder" the narrator's military fantasies are presented as a very questionable form of escapism: not only are they wildly unrealistic, they reflect the same masochistic tendencies that already cripple him.

However, even as he censures the "little soldier's" actions, the stranger does not presume to judge his dreams, only hinting gently that fantasy may be preferable to fulfillment. He does not presume to know the boy's sorrow, pain and loneliness, or even to know how best to address him. It is the cautiousness of the stranger's message that makes this "the only time a person spoke to me as if to a person."

Ungar uses the very limitations of language, voice and perspective to convey the melancholy indefinability inherent in the human experience, the subjective construction of reality which is a source of torment but also, paradoxically, of comfort and dignity.

I would like to thank the following people and institutions without whom this translation would not have come about: Dirk Stamm, for introducing me to Hermann Ungar; the Stiftung Kulturfonds, for enabling me to work on the translation in the stimulating atmosphere and sea breezes of Künstlerhaus Lukas in Ahrenshoop; Professor Nancy Wingfield, for explaining to me what a "health book" is.

I would also like to express my appreciation for Dr. Dieter Sudhoff's groundbreaking work on Ungar; all citations of secondary sources in this afterword are from his book *Hermann Ungar: Leben-Werk-Wirkung.*

Isabel F. Cole
Berlin, 2006

COMMENTARY & SOURCES

Boys & Murderers

First published as *Knaben und Mörder. Zwei Erzählungen* (Leipzig / Wien / Zurich: E.P. Tal u. Co, 1920). A Czech translation appeared in 1926.

A MAN AND A MAID

Originally titled "Ein Mann und eine Magd," the story takes place in Boskovice and various cities in the United States. While the American locations are described only schematically, the scenes in Boskovice are detailed and actual. The Jewish Town of Boskovice administered a charity house that served as joint orphanage and home for the elderly (its wards were three orphans and three elderly). The hospice was endowed by Nathan Löw-Beer, a local industrialist, and stood near the main synagogue with its courtyard abutting the Christian houses on the market square. Its outer appearance is described in detail in the story, while the house's interior is also actual with some details borrowed from Ungar's own home "Kaiser-Haus" (Na Císařské). It was customary for a stone bench to be situated in front of many Jewish homes. The game of balls and buttons belongs to Ungar's childhood. The director of the hospice, who in the story is named Mayer (after Josef Mayer, Ungar's teacher at the Jewish school), was in reality Samuel Zobel, who, easily recognizing himself in the story, took umbrage at how he was portrayed. The elderly ward Jelínek was named after Ignác Jelínek, who actually lived opposite the house around 1900. The Bell inn is in reality The Golden Grape, which one could enter through the back garden with its grove of walnut trees, which were cut down after the Second World War. The inn mentioned by the narrator upon his return from America was indeed built after the First World War and is today's Hotel Slavia.

STORY OF A MURDER

Originally titled "Geschichte eines Mordes," it is set solely in Boskovice. The main character lives with his father in a house by the church that was still standing after the Second World War on the north side of the market square and corresponds to Ungar's description. The traveler's inn is again The Golden Grape, which was a coach station. A hunchbacked barber actually worked in the barbershop on the square. Ungar devised the name of Josef Haschek from Josef Schweik and the author of *The Good Soldier Schweik*, Jaroslav Hašek. Even the pendulum clocks describyed by the narrator could indeed be seen on the square in the shop window of the clockmaker Alois Vasíř.

Colbert's Journey

First published as *Colberts Reise. Erzählungen* (Berlin: Ernst Rowohlt, 1930), the volume came out posthumously with a remarkably emotive preface by Thomas Mann (reprinted in this volume). The publisher's editor made the selection of stories, the majority of which had been published during Ungar's lifetime in various periodicals (save "The Wine-Traveler," "Alexander," and "Reasons for Everything"). Much of Ungar's unpublished work was lost after the author's death, and particularly after 1938.

COLBERT'S JOURNEY

First published as "Colberts Reise. Erzählung" in *Die Neue Rundschau*, 8/33 (Berlin: August 1922). The character Modlizki appears later in the novel *Die Klasse* [The Class] and in the comedy *Die Gartenlaube* [The Arbor], which with minor deviations has the same plot as this story. The French-sounding name "Colbert" personifies the overall behavior of the main character, although the Kolbert surname is found in present-day Boskovice as well. Ungar's mother, Jeanetta, was fascinated by France and the French language, and, striking up a friendship with the local aristocracy, she often visited Countess Mensdorff-Pouilly at the château to converse in French and to listen to French radio.

THE WINE-TRAVELER

First published as "Der Weinreisende. Erzählung" in *Die Neue Rundschau*, 2/41 (Berlin: February 1930). Written in the first person, the protagonist is not named. The opening part is borrowed from an earlier story, "The Caliph" (see below). The narrator speaks of his father having led a double life and states in conclusion that he does as well: as an upstanding citizen and as a murderer whose crime has gone unpunished. The story is set in Prague.

REASONS FOR EVERYTHING

First published posthumously as "Die Bewandtnis" in *Die literarische Welt*, 5 (Berlin: December 19, 1929), edited by Willy Haas, who had been given the story by Camill Hoffmann from Ungar's papers.

TULPE

First published as "Tulpe" in *Berliner Tageblatt*, 54, no. 431 (September 11, 1925). The surname "Tulpe" means tulip, but it also has resonances with the Czech colloquial expression for dunce, "ťulpas," which itself is derived from the German "Tölpel." This secondary meaning fits the story's satiric tone.

ALEXANDER (A FRAGMENT)

First published as "Alexander. Fragment" in *Jüdischer Almanach auf das Jahr 5691 (1930/31)* (Prague: 1930). Though it appeared posthumously, it might very well be the opening chapter to a working version of a novel that was to be set in Boskovice. If this is indeed the case, this fragment is all that remains of the manuscript. The names Chlup and Svátek were common in Boskovice at that time. The suicide of Wenzel Svatek, who hangs himself on a "slender sapling," references the suicide of Ungar's classmate Štěpán Suchý. The mention of the Cyril and Methodius statue at the entrance to Boskovice corresponds in detail to reality. Alexander's account of his rich Jewish classmate who attends piano lessons is actually a reference to the young Ungar himself, who took piano from a Mr. Slovák on Komenský Street. Finally, the description of the storehouse as well as Alexander's father's work at the Jewish merchant's is an exact description of the Ungar house.

MELLON, THE "ACTOR"

First published as "Mellon, der 'Schauspieler' " in *Prager Tagblatt,* 54, no. 124 (May 28, 1929). The main character is based on Ungar's classmate, Karl Blum, at the II. German State Gymnasium in Brno. According to Ungar's roommate, Alexander Loebl, Blum, who was severely handicapped, wanted to become an actor and would annoy his fellow students with his incessant recitations.

BOBEK MARRIES

First published as "Bobek heiratet" in *Berliner Tagblatt,* 56, no. 228 (May 15, 1928, Morgen-Ausgabe). The story was written around the same time as the humorous sections of chapters 5, 6, and 12 from *The Class.* Bertolt Brecht used this text (not Hašek's *Schweik*) for the eighth scene of his *Schweik in the Second World War.*

THE SECRET WAR

First published as "Der heimliche Krieg" in *Prager Tagblatt*, 54, no. 155 (July 4, 1929). The despised teacher named only by the initial R. has been identified as Romuald Rinesch, the math teacher at the Brno Gymnasium. Loebl describes Rinesch as pitiful and seriously neurotic, suffering from an inferiority complex and having a fear of his students, who didn't respect him in turn. Loebl also suspects that Rinesch is the model for the teacher Blau in *The Class*. Written in the first person, the story is clearly autobiographical. Ungar likely borrowed the narrator's sudden fainting spells in school from his Uncle Max, who in his memoirs recounts just such episodes.

THE BROTHERS

First published as "Die Brüder" in *Berliner Börsen-Courier*, 57, no. 385 (August 17, 1924). This story was deliberately placed at the close of the collection, and it could be called Ungar's "emblematic" story in that it is based on a real event. Hermann and his younger brother Felix met at the train station in Brno. They took the evening train to Skalice nad Svitavou. The local line to Boskovice had been laid in 1908, but around midnight there was no connection. So they walked rather than wait for the hired coach. First they passed the mill at the edge of Skalice (known as "Virnitz"), then they walked through another village, Mladkov, where they heard the dogs barking in Svitávka (which Ungar calls Vintavka). The hollow road that plays such an important part in the story actually existed until after the Second World War. Ungar has the Rovná hill located to the left of the road. It actually lies to the right of the road (in the direction of Boskovice) and is still a popular destination for walks and outings.

SANATORIUM

First published as "Heilanstalt" in *Prager Tagblatt*, 44 (July 13, 1919). This was Ungar's first published work of prose. Readers might be reminded of the sanatorium from Thomas Mann's *Magic Mountain*, which appeared in 1924. Ungar much admired Mann's work and read the novel as soon as it came out. He wrote Mann an enthusiastic letter in which he makes a startling confession: "I am not sure it's possible for one to read about horrible things without himself being overcome with horror." This might have been Ungar's reaction to his critics who claimed that his portrayal of humankind were so gruesome that one became terrified when reading it.

LETTER TO A WOMAN

First published as "Brief an eine Frau" in *Prager Tagblatt*, 44 (November 23, 1919). Dieter Sudhoff has remarked that this story is based on one of Ungar's experiences while living in a simple student's room on Widerhofergasse 5/11 in Vienna's 9th district, where he stayed from February 20 to April 26, 1918 while preparing for his exams at Prague University. He resided at this address on numerous occasions.

A DREAM

First published as "Traum" in *Berliner Börsen-Courier*, 54 (December 25, 1921). The disjointedness of the prose heightens its surrealistic effect as flashes of Ungar's childhood experiences in Boskovice progressively surface in separate illogical passages. The beginning is itself a continuation of an ongoing dream, and to what it is connected and who is being talked about remain unknown as the dream sequence opens. Following in quick succession are the interior of the local château's halls (where Ungar used to visit as a child), then the Ungars' kitchen, playing with his brother Felix, Christ, the professor and exams at Gymnasium, the uprising of sailors in Sevastopol (thus dating the dream), again the Cyril and Methodius monument, the brickworks nearby it, the well in the Jewish Quarter (Vážná studna), Lysice, Mayer, the teacher at the Jewish school in Boskovice, the Perná estate on the "Kaiser Road" on the way to Černá Hora, Felix standing on the balcony of the Ungar house ("Kaiser-Haus"), again the motif of his classmate's suicide "on the bastion" at Boskovice Castle, the mill motif, the railway, members of the family (Grandmother, Father, Uncle Max). Everything in Boskovice is authentic. The pond at Červená zahrada [Red Garden] was the town's swimming hole. Today the area is a sports complex. The fire engines of the Jewish firemen were famous.

BIBA IS DYING

First published as "Biba stirbt" in *Morgenzeitung und Handelsblatt* (Moravská Ostrava, December 29, 1925). The motif of a father's love for his son is common in Ungar's work and anticipates the scene in *The Class* of Blau with his newborn son.

LITTLE LIES (DIALOGUE FOR A MARRIED COUPLE)

First published as "Kleine Lügen. Dialog zwischen Eheleuten" in *Prager Tagblatt*, 52, no. 238 (October 7, 1927). This evidently takes place in Berlin (Uhlandstrasse).

THE CALIPH

First published as "Der Kalif" in *Der Freihafen*, 11, no. 2 (Hamburg: 1928/29). The story is narrated by a traveling sweets salesman and was later used by Ungar for "The Wine-Traveler." The narrator in each leads a double life. In this story he is the greatest statesman of his time in addition to his profession, even though no one realizes it. Ungar led a double life himself: he was known as a successful diplomat and good-natured companion while only very few knew that he was the author of deeply philosophical and largely pessimistic works of fiction.

compiled by Jaroslav Bránský

NOTES

p. 106 *spoke of Benedek*: Ludwig August Ritter von Benedek (1804-1871), Austrian general who lost the Battle of Königgrätz (today's Hradec Králové) to the Prussians, resulting in Austria's defeat in the Austro-Prussian War. Also known as the Battle of Sadowa (Sadová), it took place on July 3, 1866 in northeast Bohemia and was the bloodiest of the war.

p. 146 *In the year '66*: The year of the Austro-Prussian War, or Seven Weeks' War, deliberately provoked by Prussian chancellor Otto von Bismarck in an attempt to oust Austria from the German Confederation and unify Germany under Prussian dominance.

p. 148 *Harun al-Rashid*: (also known as Aaron the Upright) ca. 763 – 809. The fifth Abbasid caliph, he ruled from 786 to 809 and was renowned for his magnificent palace in Baghdad. Both he and his court were immortalized in *One Thousand and One Arabian Nights*.

p. 192 *had her in their health book*: In 19th-century Bohemia, prostitutes were required to register and carry a health book that contained the records of their medical examinations.

p. 210 *at Sevastopol in the sailors' mutiny*: A rebellion of sailors took place in 1905 in Sevastopol, an important Russian port and naval base on the Black Sea.

p. 225 *thus sparing hundreds of thousands in 1870*: The Franco-Prussian War of July 19, 1870 – May 10, 1871. Provoked by Bismarck, Prussian victory in the conflict signaled the rise of German military power.

ABOUT THE AUTHOR

Hermann Ungar was born on April 20, 1893 to a comfortable Jewish family in the small Moravian town of Boskovice, then part of the Austro-Hungarian Empire. Formerly the Jewish ghetto, the Jewish Town of Boskovice had the unusual distinction of having been established as its own municipality in 1848 (one of only two such instances, this status lasted until 1919) after the Habsburg's emancipation of the Jews in the Czech Lands. The newly founded town thus had its own mayor, police and fire department. Ungar's grandfather, Herrmann [*sic*], was the Jewish Town's de facto first mayor (as representative of Count Mensdorff-Pouilly), and his father Emil, who took over the family's distilling business, served as mayor from 1903 to 1905. Though Boskovice was largely Catholic, Jews made up approximately one-third of the total population at the beginning of the twentieth century.

It was Herrmann who expanded the family business and built the family home (known as Kaiser-Haus, or Na Císařské) where his grandchildren were born. The Ungars became one of the most prominent families in the town and were known for their strict observance of Jewish tradition. Ungar grew up speaking German and Czech, but was educated solely in the former, considered at the time more useful for achieving higher social status. Though registered at the German Jewish school, he and his younger brother, Felix, and sister, Gertrude, were largely schooled at home by a private tutor; all three later graduated from the German Gymnasium in Brno, where Hermann was top of his class. Ungar was known as an all-around student, excelling both at soccer and piano; it was also at this time that he began dabbling in literature by writing plays. Having literary ambitions himself, his father supported these efforts.

Ungar was said to have played a significant role in Czech Zionism through his skills as an organizer and the force of his personality. While at school in Brno he was a member of the Jewish students' club Veritas, and was also a member of a similar club in Boskovice called Lätitia. His involvement in these groups likely helped him to confront the Catholic bigotry (largely anti-Semitic) prevalent in the Moravian countryside. Such attitudes often found expression in deep-seated superstitions such as the "blood libel," and they also found their way into his writing (in *The Maimed*, Franz Polzer serves as a repository for all the superstitions Ungar associated with his native region). During Ungar's adolescence the Hilsner trial was still fresh in people's minds (Leopold Hilsner, wrongly accused of ritually murdering a Czech girl, was later defended by Tomáš G. Masaryk, first president of Czechoslovakia) as were the attacks on Jewish shops and homes in the countryside it precipitated. And then in 1918, right at war's end, a pogrom erupted in Holešov (also in Moravia) during which two Jews were killed.

The Veritas group would meet to discuss Jewish history and the Zionist movement and read Jewish newspapers, which inspired Ungar to begin intensive study of the Old Testament as well as Hebrew and Arabic at Friedrich Wilhelm University (now Humboldt) in Berlin from 1911 to 1912. While in Berlin, he became a member of another Zionist youth group, Hasmonäa, and continued to write stories and novels. These early literary efforts have been lost.

In 1912 Ungar transferred to the university in Munich to study law, ultimately continuing at the Law Faculty in Prague. The Great War came, and Ungar volunteered for service in an artillery unit of the Austro-Hungarian army. Finding himself on the Russian front, he was wounded and in 1916 was back in Brno in the hospital with a Silver Medal of Valor. After convalescing, he returned to Prague to finish his studies, earning his law doctorate in 1918. No longer interested in Zionism, his allegiance was now to the democratic ideals of Masaryk's Czechoslovak Republic. Subsequent time in 1918 as a clerk in a Prague law firm led him to realize he did not want to be either a lawyer or a judge, so in 1919 he accepted a position as dramaturge and actor in the Municipal Theater of Cheb, the far western outpost of the new republic.

Ungar's writing career officially began in 1920 with the publication of *Boys & Murderers*, a book that not only caught the attention of Thomas Mann, but was also highly praised by the director Berthold Viertel. In the meantime, he had become a clerk at a German trade bank in Prague, a post he resigned in 1921 to become foreign trade attaché at the Czechoslovak Embassy in Berlin. Here he became friends with the press attaché, Camill Hoffmann, who in his younger days had been a Decadent poet associated with Paul Leppin's group Jung-Prag. In 1922 Ungar married Margaret Weiss (Hoffmann was his best man), who was from a Prague Jewish family, and in 1923 their first son, Michael, was born.

Also in 1922 the first chapter of *The Maimed* appeared under the title "The Bank Clerk" in Otto Pick's anthology *Deutsche Erzähler aus der Tschechoslowakei* [German Writers from Czechoslovakia]. The book was under consideration by Kurt Wolff, Franz Kafka's publisher, who though he admired the novel was afraid of being brought up on obscenity charges if he published it. Ungar also had his doubts, but in the end he withdrew *The Maimed* from Wolff and gave it to Ernst Rowohlt, who brought it out in 1923. This was followed by a slim work of reportage, *Die Ermordung des Hauptmanns Hanika* [The Murder of Captain Hanik; 1925], and the publication of his only other novel, *The Class*, in 1927. The following year he was transferred back to Prague where he was given the position of "ministerial commissar." In 1929 his second son, Alexander, was born, and Ungar resigned his post due to failing health and a desire to end his "double life" by devoting himself entirely to his writing.

At the time of his illness, Ungar had been planning a trip to Palestine to visit his sister, who had emigrated in 1926 and was working as a doctor in Tel Aviv. The trip never came off as his condition forced him into the hospital with acute appendicitis. Having the operation too late — Ungar was a notorious hypochondriac and apparently the doctors did not take his complaints seriously — he died at the age of thirty-six on October 28, 1929. He is buried in the small Jewish section of Prague's Malvazinka Cemetery.

His wife and two sons immigrated to England before Nazi Germany occupied the country. His father died in Boskovice in 1941 and is buried in the town's Jewish cemetery in an unmarked grave. According to Jewish custom, a gravestone is not erected until one year has passed, and by that time Boskovice's Jews had been deported. Ungar's mother and brother and his brother's entire family died in the concentration camps. His sister in Palestine committed suicide in 1946 when she learned of their fate.

Two of Ungar's works appeared posthumously. In December 1929 his play *Die Gartenlaube* [The Arbor] was performed at the Theater am Schiffbauerdamm in Berlin. It was published the following year by Ernst Rowohlt, as was the short-story collection *Colbert's Journey*, which Thomas Mann called a "minor masterpiece" in his preface to the book. Ungar saw his two novels and some shorter prose published in Czech translation during his life, and it was something he attached great importance to, writing one of his translators, Jan Grmel: "A Czech translation means more for me than for any other non-Czech author, because when I write I have the feeling that I would like to and should write in Czech." And in 1928 Gallimard published a French translation of *The Maimed* (and later *Boys & Murderers*). Yet despite this attention, the Czech daily *Literární noviny* was justified in writing in 1932: "One of the most talented young German authors (from Moravia) died not too long ago. Hermann Ungar hasn't had much luck here. Prague publishers have put out his books in editions that hardly anyone notices and are soon forgotten." Indeed, Ungar's work was then forgotten for decades.

New interest was briefly sparked by the now legendary Kafka conferences in 1963 and 1965 at Liblice Castle north of Prague where Ungar was included as a member of the "Prague circle." Johannes Urzidil made numerous mentions of Ungar along with Ernst Weiss and Ludwig Winder as three Moravian Jewish writers who made their own particular contributions to Prague German literature. And in addition to Camill Hoffman and Weiss, Ungar counted among his friends some of Prague's most famous German-Jewish writers: Paul Kornfeld, Franz Werfel, and Egon Erwin Kisch. Even so, Max Brod, who canonized the list of writers associated with the Prague circle, mentions Ungar only in passing with the excuse that he really couldn't remember much about him. Brod's lapse of memory is curious in that he admits to having likely encountered Ungar at the *Prager Tagblatt*'s editorial offices and that Ungar even dedicated his first book to him, a work he thought "banal." But what also seems to have escaped his memory is that he actually wrote a eulogy to Ungar that associated him with the Prague circle. The fact remains, however, that Ungar and Kafka never met, and for Brod the "circle" was defined by its center.

Any effort to resurrect Ungar's work ended after the Soviet invasion of Czechoslovakia in 1968 and the institution of a neo-Stalinist regime that brought an end to any form of independent culture. But in Germany and Austria new editions began to appear in the 1980s, and German television aired dramatizations of *The Class* and *The Arbor*. The past fifteen years have seen the most activity with new reprints as well as translations appearing in a number of languages. Dieter Sudhoff published his major monograph on Ungar in 1990 and edited the three volumes of his collected work (published 2001-2002). Importantly, in Ungar's native land two volumes of his complete works have finally been published in Czech.

ABOUT THE TRANSLATOR

Isabel Fargo Cole is a graduate of the University of Chicago and has lived in Berlin for over a decade. Her translations have appeared in a number of publications, such as *Archipelago*, *Agni*, *Antioch*, *Chicago Review*, and *Prague Literary Review*. On the board of the Berlin literary forum and magazine lauter niemand, she is currently organizing *no man's land*, an English-language magazine of new German writing.

Boys & Murderers
Hermann Ungar

Translated from the German by Isabel Fargo Cole

Preface by Thomas Mann reprinted with
the kind permission of Fischer Verlag.
Cover and frontispiece by Otto Gutfreund
courtesy of the Jewish Museum in Prague.
Set in Garamond Semibold
Design by Infinity Dreamscapes

First published in English in 2006 by
TWISTED SPOON PRESS
P.O. Box 21–Preslova 12, 150 21 Prague 5, Czech Republic
(info@twistedspoon.com / www.twistedspoon.com)

Printed and bound in the Czech Republic
by PBtisk, Příbram

Distributed to the trade in North America by
SCB DISTRIBUTORS
15608 South New Century Drive, Gardena, CA 90248-2129
1-800-729-6423 / info@scbdistributors.com / www.scbdistributors.com

Thanks are due Allie Wilding for her comments on the manuscript and
Jaroslav Bránský for allowing the use of his notes on Ungar's work.